The Man in Bearskin

The Man in Bearskin

J. Keuning

Rewritten by **Cobie Bos**

BAKER BOOK HOUSE
Grand Rapids, Michigan 49506

Paperback edition copyright 1982
by Baker Book House Company

ISBN: 0-8010-5448-6

Printed in the United States of America

1

The warm June sun had sunk into the waters of Lake Michigan and a fresh breeze had sprung up out of the west. To the group of Holland immigrants camped on the east shore where the Black River pours its waters into the great lake, the fresh air was a welcome change from the stifling heat of the day. The tired travelers welcomed the chance to sleep in comfort, so they quickly settled down for the night in the crude, hastily constructed shack which was their camp.

Two men of the company were still awake. Because of the refreshing breeze blowing in from the lake, they had decided to remain outside a little longer, rather than to join their companions in the shack where the air was warm and close. They sat on the sand, resting their backs against the wall of the shelter, talking about the trying experiences which they and their comrades had undergone in their journey from the Netherlands, and, now that they had nearly arrived at their destination, they also spoke of their plans and their hopes for a happy future.

Neither of the men noticed the silent form which emerged from the black forest along the shore and made its way across the narrow stretch of sand toward the rude building. In the darkness it might have been mistaken for a bear, for those great animals were plentiful in that region. Yet, it seemed too small for a bear, and it moved too quickly.

The figure that left the deep shade of the forest now stood, hesitant, in the open light of the beach. It was a man. On his head he wore a dark hood-like cap, and joined to this, across his shoulders, hung a cape of the same color. It was a great bearskin garment, cut in the style of a parka. The face of the stranger was hidden in a huge black beard; the heavy mass of hair swept down to his chest. The strange dress and secretive actions of the night visitor surrounded him with an air of mystery and suggested that he was on an unusual errand.

A short distance from the hut he stopped as if to listen. He had heard the voices of the two men in earnest conversation. Stealthily he sidled over to the opposite wall and with eager ears strained to catch the drift of the talk between the two. He was so close that he could understand their conversation. He heard them speak of the long ocean voyage in the steerage of a sailing vessel, of the tedious journey from Albany to Buffalo in horse-drawn canal boats, of the lake trip in rough waters, of their bright hopes for the future when they would finally join the immigrants who had already founded the village of Holland.

After a while one of the men said, "Well, Gerrit, don't you think we had better retire?"

"I think we might as well, Hendrik," replied the other. "Let's see if there is any room for us inside. I'm glad that my wife and children, at least, have a place to sleep. The rest will do them a world of good."

4

The eavesdropper heard the two men rise and start around the corner of the building. He knew he would surely be discovered. His only chance was to bolt for the woods.

"Listen! What's that?" whispered Gerrit in an excited voice as the stranger made his first move in the direction of the forest.

It was too late for the stranger to withdraw. He stood plainly visible before the two men. Crouching low, he turned and, resisting the urge to run, stalked toward cover.

"It's a bear," whispered Hendrik, deceived by the cloak of bearskin.

"A bear! Maybe, but a two-legged one," said Gerrit. "Don't you see it's walking on two legs?"

"That's right! It's a thief who thought we were all sleeping."

"I think you're right. Shall we follow him?"

Hendrik sprang into action. He ran across the beach at full speed until he had almost caught up with the fleeing figure. The stranger didn't realize that he was being chased until Hendrik was almost upon him. Shocked, he made a sudden dash for the trees. In doing so, he let go of his bearskin cape, and it fell to the ground. Before Hendrik could overtake him, he was swallowed up in the forest.

The two immigrants hesitated to follow. They were not acquainted with these dark and dense woods. Besides, their shadowy visitor made them uneasy. But Hendrik had noticed that the man's cape had fallen from his shoulders, and after they searched for a few minutes, Gerrit found it on the ground.

"Here, I have it," he called, "but what sort of a

thing is it? It's a skin of some kind and it's still warm."

"That's it," said Hendrik, "that's the thief's cape."

"Thief! Robber!" cried Gerrit. "We don't want your filthy skin. We'll hang it on a limb, and if you want it, come and get it. But see to it that you don't come near this shack again."

"Gerrit, old man," Hendrik laughed, "why yell at him that way? He doesn't understand Dutch anyway. He's probably an American."

"Or an Indian," added Gerrit, somewhat sheepishly.

"Very probably," continued Hendrik, "but let's forget about him and get some sleep. He's too frightened to return any more tonight."

The two left the bearskin on a small bush near which it had fallen and returned to their companions, none of whom seemed to have been awakened by the disturbance. In a little while they had settled themselves among the sleepers.

But sleep did not come easily to Gerrit Kolf. He was disturbed by what had happened that night. He tossed about restlessly. He knew that life in this new land would be so different for him and his family. It was the beginning of a whole new life, and he feared for the future.

Gerrit was a member of the second group of Hollanders to come to this region. Earlier, in September of 1846, a band of fifty-three Dutchmen, together with their leader, Dominie A. C. Van Raalte, had set sail from Rotterdam in the brig *Southerner*. They were the first of hundreds of poor, needy Dutch folk who immigrated to the United States. They came looking for a chance to make a better living, and

6

hoping, too, that in this new land they would be able to worship God freely.

For seven long weeks this band of sincere Christians endured their poor quarters on the ship, cooking their own food, sleeping where and how they could, worshiping God in their own way with prayers and psalms and sermons. Finally, they landed at New York where they were cared for by friends whom they found among the Dutch-Americans of that city.

The question of where to settle now faced the leader, Dominie Van Raalte. Winter was coming soon. The party sailed by steamer to Albany, went from there to Buffalo by train, and then by boat to Detroit.

With the help of several kind Americans, especially Judge Kellogg of Allegan, Van Raalte was able to look over several regions of Michigan in order to find a suitable site for his colony. The region near the mouth of Black River on the east coast of Lake Michigan appealed very strongly to him. It had a good harbor and many opportunities for trade. Also, there was a magnificent stand of timber which would provide the first settlers with homes and a plentiful supply of fuel.

Van Raalte purchased from the government a large tract of land at the head of what is now called Black Lake, and to this wild region, in the winter of 1847, came a small band of sturdy Hollanders eager to make a home for themselves and to provide opportunities for their children.

The first winter was like the one experienced by the original settlers of Plymouth. The colonists knew nothing of the woodsman's craft; yet great trees had to be felled to clear the land, shelters had to be built

7

to house their families, food had to be provided to satisfy their needs. But they were so sure that it had been right for them to come to America, so sure that God would care for them, that they began their task with boundless energy. Before long they had cleared a small area of land and had built themselves rude huts of logs and hemlock boughs.

They called their settlement Holland. They believed that their infant colony would become a refuge for other persecuted Hollanders and a strong, wealthy community in the commonwealth of Michigan.

The first settlers knew that many would follow them to their little village, and in order to make their reception as welcome and comfortable as possible, they decided to build a shelter on the shores of Lake Michigan at the mouth of Black Lake, where steamers could land future colonists coming by boat from Buffalo or Detroit. Accordingly, a group of men, equipped with a few tools and a handful of nails, built from driftwood the rude shack where Gerrit Kolf and his friends now were housed.

Gerrit tried to sleep, but his mind was too busy. He recalled the picture he had had of America while he was still in the Netherlands. A friend who had left earlier for America had written Gerrit that the soil was rich, there was plenty of food, there were endless opportunities to make a good living, and the settlers were free to worship God according to their beliefs. Now he thought of what had really taken place, of the terrible voyage, of the steady diet of bread, pork, and coffee, of the harsh treatment they had received from the canal boat crew during the long trip to Buffalo, of the bare beaches of the great

8

lake on which they lay, of the gloomy forest behind them with which they would have to struggle for food and shelter.

His fair picture of the village of Holland with board houses, paved streets, stores, and lights, had been shattered by the tale of the man in charge of the affairs of the newcomers to the settlement. Gerrit learned from him that there were no houses, but only log huts built without windows and without floors, drafty and cold in the winter. He learned that there were no roads, no stores, no lights, and that food was scarce. When he thought of these things and considered his frail wife and four children, his courage began to fail, and for a moment he was sorry that he had ever left the Netherlands.

But Gerrit was a God-fearing man. He had entered on his great adventure because the government of his homeland refused him freedom of worship. He had put his trust in his Heavenly Father. Now he talked with his God in prayer. His drooping courage was restored by the thought of God's almighty power, and he found himself so quieted that he fell asleep.

Scarcely had he dozed off when he was awakened by an unusual sound near the hut. Instantly he was fully alert. But he heard only the heavy breathing of the sleepers and the restless grunts of those who were uncomfortable on their beds of sand. Very quietly he arose and stationed himself at the wall nearest which he had first heard the sound. His straining ears caught the crunching noise of a footfall on the sand. Another followed, and another. Something was cautiously approaching the building.

"Has the thief come back?" thought Gerrit. "Would

he dare to return to the beach after having been chased away once? Poor as we are, we seem to be haunted by trouble. The little we have someone is trying to take from us."

But the footsteps stopped. The thief had paused to listen. Was he alarmed? Had he detected any commotion in the cabin? Gerrit was at a loss what to do. So bold a thief should be caught and punished. But Gerrit doubted his ability to catch him alone. To awaken his friends would be to warn the intruder and allow him to escape. Perhaps it was better to first make sure who the stranger was and what he wanted. Perhaps, after all, it was not a man but some roaming animal attracted to the encampment by the scent of food.

Now Gerrit heard a new sound outside, the sound of something heavy being dragged toward the hut. "The thief is at our baggage," he thought in terror. "He's dragging away one of our chests to open it at his leisure in the woods. I'll awaken Hendrik and we'll catch the robber in the very act." Suddenly the noise of the dragging ceased, and the sound of retreating footsteps suggested the hasty departure of the unwelcome guest.

Gerrit was too alarmed to be inactive any longer. He didn't know whether any of their belongings were departing with the visitor, but he wished to make sure of it immediately. He stumbled his way to the opening of the shelter and stepped outside. The moon had risen and the beach was lighted with a pale silver. Gerrit saw a hurrying figure disappear into the ghostlike line of trees along the shore, but he could not tell so quickly if it was a man or a beast.

"It's the same fellow who was here before," Gerrit

thought, for he had seen the bearskin hood and cape. "What does he want around here, anyway? If he has come to steal, why should he leave so quickly when there is nothing to alarm him?"

Gerrit's curiosity was not easily satisfied. He went around to the side of the building where he had heard the queer dragging sound. Unfortunately, the shadow of the building made it difficult to see objects near the shack. Yet Gerrit was certain that a dark, shapeless thing lay on the sand close to the shelter. It seemed large and terrible, and Gerrit's heart was filled with the fear that he might encounter an unfriendly bear or wolf. For a full moment he stood intently studying the mysterious object before him.

Its inaction reassured him. No wild beast would have lain so still for so long a time unless it were asleep. Again, he was certain that the object had been dragged there, and even though he understood little about wildlife, he knew that no beast permits itself to be dragged about if it is able to prevent it. Encouraged by these thoughts, he neared the object until he was only a foot or two from it.

Timidly he kicked it. It was soft and fleshy, but motionless. He dared not reach down with his hand to feel of it, but with a piece of driftwood he began to prod it. He observed a thin leg protuding from the heap. Summoning up his courage, he grasped the leg and pulled the object into the light of the moon.

He fully expected a man or wild beast to spring from under the covering of animal hide and attack him. As it was, the mass of darkness did not move. From its antlers Gerrit knew it was a deer.

11

"So!" he sighed, greatly relieved. "A dead deer! Who could have guessed it? I've heard that venison is good to eat, and we'll make good use of this fellow. But how did it get here, and why was it brought?"

As if to find an answer to his question, he looked down at the dead form before him. There, fastened to the antlers of the buck, was a piece of paper. Eagerly he seized it, hoping to find an explanation for all these strange happenings. Something was written on it, but the light of the moon was too dim for him to read it.

Hurrying to the heap of ashes left from last night's fire, he poked at the embers until they glowed. A few sticks of wood were soon ablaze. By the light of the flames he could see that the writing was clear and bold.

How wonderful! The message was written in his own native language! A message written in Dutch, delivered on the horns of a buck by a mysterious messenger on the barren shore of Lake Michigan! Gerrit was aflame with excitement. With trembling voice he read aloud the contents of the message:

This deer is a gift to Gerrit Kolf, his wife, and four children. He called me a thief. It is true, I am a thief, but I steal from no one. This is in payment for my cape. Gerrit Kolf will hear more of me.

THE MAN IN BEARSKIN

He read and reread the brief note. Astonishment was painted in every line of his face. When he had practically learned the message by heart, he sat staring into the flickering blaze and wondered. A hundred questions leaped to his mind, questions to

12

which he could find no answer. Who could have written the note? Someone, surely, who knew the Dutch language. How did the writer know Gerrit's name? And how could he have known Gerrit had a wife and four children? He had been called a thief, but he seemed to take no offense. In fact, he called himself a thief! And Gerrit was to hear more of him! Was this a promise of good, or of evil? The gift of the buck seemed to show a friendly spirit, but why should the gift have been made to him, Gerrit, personally? Why should the giver feel obliged to Gerrit? Why had he signed himself "The Man in Bearskin"?

For a long while Gerrit was puzzled, and he made no move to return to sleep. It was some time before he noticed that the fire had gone out and that he was sitting alone on the chilling sand of the shore. He arose and entered the shelter. But sleep was impossible after so strange an event. He dozed restlessly, disturbed by wild dreams, starting at the sound of a creaking limb or the groan of a sleeper.

It was not long before the breaking dawn colored the sky and spread its light over the forest. Gerrit could hardly wait for full sunup before he went out on the beach to examine once more the deer that had been given him so mysteriously. There it lay, harmless and still, a splendid buck, waiting only to be skinned, divided, and roasted, to delight the hungry immigrants.

The presence of the animal aroused keen curiosity among the now-awakened travelers. The events of the night were told, the strange message was passed from hand to hand, and all sorts of fantastic explanations were offered, but none satisfied Gerrit. There was one person who volunteered a little information which made the events seem more believable. The man sent from the village of Holland to direct immigrants to their destination said that he had heard of "The Man in Bearskin."

"I've heard of the man," he said. "Some of the people of the village have told me that there is a strange person who wears a bearskin cape, roams about the forest, lives in the deepest part of it, but harms no one. We can't get close enough to see who he is, and we do not know why he lives as he does. We call him 'The Man in Bearskin.'"

This bit of information only increased Gerrit's anxiety and curiosity. Why had he been singled out from the whole company? Was someone playing a joke on him? Was some great evil coming upon him, some disaster that he could not prevent? His mind was troubled and confused. His courage was turning to fear and hopelessness.

None of the group of campers had any reason to be jealous of Gerrit because the buck was presented to him. The deer was skinned in a rude fashion by the unskilled Hollanders and roasted over an open fire. The whole company helped in the preparation. When the venison was ready for eating, a prayer was offered to God and a blessing asked on the food. The band of hungry immigrants eagerly pitched into the meal and fully enjoyed the gracious gift of the mysterious stranger who called himself "The Man in Bearskin."

2

Gerrit Kolf did not remain long at the landing place on the shore of the lake. He was quick to observe that it would be some time before the entire company could be transported with their luggage to the little village six miles inland on Black Lake.

When a timber raft carrying beams and planks bound for Holland from the Kalamazoo River appeared at the inlet, Gerrit made arrangements with the man in charge to bring his family and goods to the city. Gerrit agreed to help with the work during the journey. He was eager to see with his own eyes the site of his future home, even though he knew there would be disappointments.

Gerrit loaded the chests of baggage on the odd craft and found a place for his wife and four children. There were other families who were eager to get aboard, but the raft was too small for more than one family.

The journey was very slow. The rivermen kept the craft near the shore, and more than once they had to go over the side to free it from snags and shoals. Their progress was so slow that at dusk they were still a long way from their destination, and they had to go ashore to spend the night. The season was warm so the inexperienced campers were not uncomfortable.

It was the first night that Gerrit had ever spent in such a wild and uncivilized place. He had traveled in company with a rather large number of companions and, except for the night on the beach, had slept on shipboard or in places from which he could see houses and other buildings. But now his companions had been reduced to his family and the men who operated the raft.

The forest about him was thick and dark. The heavy stands of virgin oak, maple, and hemlock shut out the light of the moon and stars, and filled the place with the whisperings of tossing branches. Tall and straight they stood, row upon row, stretching back to form a solid wall of stately trunks—a fearsome forest. With the majestic forest at his back, the rolling waters of Black Lake at his feet, the expanse of the starry heavens about him, Gerrit knew the awful gnawing of loneliness. He longed for the open meadows of his fatherland, the shores of which he had left forever.

The cries of his youngest child aroused him from his thoughts. He forgot his own fears as he and his wife tried to comfort the child. Just to have his wife beside him, to feel her love and courage, gave Gerrit new hope as he kissed her in the stillness of the cool night.

He was the first to awake in the morning. To his surprise he found a strange object lying on the shore near the place where he had slept. It was a large sack of something, and it had not been there the night before. Filled with curiosity, he approached.

16

To the mouth of the bag was tied a note. He read it at a glance.

For Gerrit Kolf and his family, from
THE MAN IN BEARSKIN

It was written in the same language and by the same hand as the first mysterious message. The rivermen were especially surprised by the presence of the sack, but their astonishment doubled after Gerrit told them the story of the night before.

"The fellow seems to want to do good to you at least," remarked the skipper.

"So it seems," Gerrit replied. "He isn't an enemy as I first thought him to be, for he had plenty of chance to do us harm last night if he had wanted to. But why is he so eager to help us? Or is it a trick? Is he planning some horrible deed after he has set our minds at ease with these generous gifts? Let's see what he brought this time."

The sack was opened and found to contain cornmeal. "He seems to know that we are short of food," said Vrouw Kolf.

"He knows very well that there is little to be gotten in the colony," said the boatsman. "You ought to be thankful for this. It's a gift well worth receiving. You'll find yourselves in need of it before long."

The need for an early start on their journey cut short any further discussion of the matter. A hurried breakfast was eaten, the family was bundled on the raft, and the crude lumber boat was once more under way.

It was noon when the load of timber was beached at the little settlement at the head of the lake. The scene which presented itself to the wide-eyed Gerrit was by no means inviting. Trees he saw, trees, trees, trees, trees, everywhere trees. There were trees upright and fallen on all sides of him. There was a little clearing in full sunlight, but even here a thick sprinkling of stumps spoke of giant trees whose hard trunks had felt the bite of the axe. Each one of them had fallen only after many hours of hard labor. Gerrit was fearful of the day when he would have to shoulder an axe and clear an area for his first little farm. He knew nothing of woodcraft; he had not the slightest idea of how to go about felling a tree. In this respect he was like the first colonists whose awkward attempts at swinging an axe had made the Indians of the neighborhood laugh. The red men, however, were friendly and freely gave advice. They pointed out the mistakes of the settlers and showed them how to bring down the great trees with the least amount of labor. The Hollanders had plenty of opportunities to practice their new craft, and they soon became quite skillful.

The denseness of the forest cast a half shadow over the land, causing it to appear as if it were nearly dusk. The breezes blowing through the cedars and hemlocks reduced the heat from the summer sun. The fresh greens of the maples and willows added a cool touch to the scene.

Here and there among the trees stood a humble hut, the home of a first settler. The building of permanent homes had been postponed because it was more important to clear the ground so that crops could be grown to feed the colonists. Some families had to be satisfied with a shelter of boughs with a

18

canvas roof; others were fortunate enough to have a complete tent of canvas.

Even now the men of the village were busy in clearing the land. Gerrit approached a father and son who were cutting down a tree near their cabin. It was clear that the two axemen had not learned thoroughly the lesson taught by the Indians. They had not yet acquired the full, free swing of the true lumberman. They hacked and chopped at the trunk with a great deal of sweating and grunting, but the chips were small. The cutters had nearly finished chopping through the tree, but as they had cut entirely around it instead of making two notches, one on each side, they were uncertain as to just where the great hemlock was going to fall.

Just as Gerrit reached the men, the great tree swayed threateningly; the two cutters drew back with frightened haste; a shout went up. Gerrit stopped short, uncertain where to go. He looked up to see the distant top moving slowly in his direction. Very slowly at first, and then with increasing speed, the towering trunk swished through the air. Gerrit scurried to safety and watched the forest giant fall with a thud across the clearing, smashing like a bit of paper the little lean-to of the men who had felled it. Before the land had been fully cleared, many sturdy Dutchmen were to meet a sudden death under the crushing weight of some huge oak or maple, the price paid for the fair fields and fruitful harvests that would belong to their children.

Gerrit was acquainted with one family of settlers; he arranged for his family to stay with them until the arrival of the rest of the company. In the meantime he kept busy going about the colony, looking for a favorable plot of ground for his farm. But his explorations made him dissatisfied with the soil, for he noticed that it was poor and sandy. He much preferred to plant his crops in a richer, more fertile country. He decided, therefore, to wait for the arrival of his friends. With some of them he hoped to explore the surrounding regions to find a more suitable location. Meanwhile, he helped as much as he could in the clearing of the land and the building of shelters.

It was soon clear that food was scarce in the settlement. Supplies had been expected from Allegan, a well-established town some thirty miles away, but they had failed to come. Many of the colonists had nothing to eat except the game which they were able to kill in the forest. Gerrit was generous with the sack of meal which he had received and shared it with the friends with whom his family was living.

Finally the merchants arrived from Allegan with the much-needed supplies. This helped, but during the whole first year the shortage of food was a cause for great worry. There were no roads connecting the young settlement with the outside world, and all the goods had to be carried in on the back, over narrow Indian trails. The colonists were hoping and praying that their first crop would be a good one. Therefore, clearing the land was their most important work, more important even than providing shelter for their families.

Finally the company which Gerrit had left on the beach of Lake Michigan arrived. The men who came agreed with Gerrit that they should look for better land for farming. The most adventurous men were chosen for this task. Gerrit was one of them.

It was early in the morning when the handful of men set out. Dominie Van Raalte, who had encouraged and led the first group of settlers, went with them. He knew the country, and they trusted him to help them make a wise choice of good farm land.

There were no guideposts or highways through the forest. A few Indian trails, narrow, winding, rough, were the only channels of travel. Over these the explorers tramped, crossing swamps of black, oozing mud, dipping into steep ravines, fording small brooks, climbing over fallen trees, scratching their arms and legs, panting and sweating as they had never done in the meadowlands of their native country.

They had traveled for quite a distance when suddenly they came upon a small enclosure. A string of split rails, fastened between trees, shut off a small, grassy park, in the middle of which rose a small hill.

"What is this?" exclaimed one of the party. "Does someone live here?"

"None of my people," answered the Dominie. "This is the first time I've seen this place."

"Let's look around," volunteered another, and to carry out his suggestion he placed his foot on a rail as if to leap over it. A great dog, a wolfhound, rushed down the hill with furious barking. So ferocious was the dog that the whole party withdrew from the fence into the edge of the protecting woods. The hound stopped at the railing and contented himself with low growlings and an occasional bark to warn the intruders.

Certain that the dog would stay where he was, the men examined the place more closely, and to their surprise they discovered a small shelter of boughs built on the side of the hill. Through the open door of the hut, they saw a man.

He was clearly unhappy at his discovery, for he quickly arose, put on a large cap, threw a cape of animal skin about his shoulders, hurried out of the shelter, and disappeared instantly behind the trunk of a gigantic elm.

"The 'Man in Bearskin'!" exclaimed several men in unison.

"Your friend, Gerrit Kolf!" excitedly said another.

Gerrit had seen the man's strange clothing, and he believed that the bearskin cape was the one he picked up on the beach. Gerrit trembled with excitement. Now he would discover who had given him the buck and the sack of ground corn. The mystery was about to be unraveled.

The other members of the party were uncertain about what to do next. They would gladly have rested at the dwelling of this strange man, but the dog's fierceness and the odd disappearance of the man himself made them hesitant.

"Is this the home of that fellow?" Gerrit asked Dominie Van Raalte.

"I guess so," he replied. "He has the ground marked out and seems to live in that hut. But I don't know enough about the man to speak with certainty. He appeared at the village only once or twice, for what reason no one knows. He did not harm anyone and disappeared, none of us knew where. This is as much of a discovery for me as it is for you."

"It is quite unusual that he should be dressed in that great bearskin, especially on a warm day like this," observed another.

"A queer fellow, indeed! I'd like to get a close look

at him," Gerrit said. "But I'm not anxious to meet his dog," he added with a glance at the watchful beast. "What does he want with an ugly animal like that?"

"Probably for company, if he lives alone. But shall we visit him, or continue our exploration?" asked the Dominie.

"I think it's safe to go in," suggested a sturdy fellow by the name of Van Harm. "We can keep the dog at bay, and I don't think the man will object too much."

"But what if he should? He may be a dangerous character," said Gerrit, not at all certain that it was proper to trespass on the man's property, since it was clear that he wanted to avoid them.

"If he is nasty, we have all the more reason for going in. We want no dangerous men living unnoticed and unwatched near Holland." As usual Dominie Van Raalte was thinking of the welfare of his followers.

"Look, there he is again! Up that great tree!"

All eyes were turned in the direction of the elm behind which the man had disappeared. At a height of ten or twelve feet, in the crotch formed by the lowest limb, sat the "Man in Bearskin." It was plain that he was worried about his unexpected visitors, worried and angry at their presence. In his hand he grasped a rifle.

The rifle was not a very encouraging sign. It seemed best to retire from the scene and to leave the owner in full possession of his land. On the other hand, wasn't it true what the Dominie had said? A person who is so free with his gun was a very undesirable neighbor to have among them.

23

But now the man had disappeared. He had slipped from the bough and was nowhere to be seen. It appeared as if the trunk of the elm was hollow and that the mysterious person had been swallowed up in the great cavity.

"He seems to wish to avoid us! Can he be man-shy?" asked one.

"I'm going over the fence to find out who this person is. We have a fine opportunity to make his acquaintance, and I for one am not going to let it slip by. We can hold off the dog with a club. Who is going to follow me?"

As Gerrit spoke he picked up a heavy stick of dry chestnut and trimmed it down to fit his hand. Having armed himself, he placed one hand on the top rail and vaulted over the fence. He had scarcely landed on the other side when the great wolf sprang growling toward him and leaped with a snarl at his throat. Gerrit was conscious of his danger and with a skillful stroke of the club turned the furious beast from him. But the now-enraged dog was quick to return to the attack, and for a moment it seemed as if Gerrit would go down with the animal at his throat. As the great beast sprang, Gerrit swung with all his might and caught the dog squarely on the side of the jaw while he swung in mid-air. The force of the blow changed the direction of his spring, and the beast missed the man by an inch or two. Gerrit shuddered as he heard the great jaws click within a few inches of his neck. The situation was now extremely dangerous. The wolf was doubly maddened by the sharp pain of the blow. Gerrit was excited and somewhat rattled by his narrow escape.

Then the dog did a most unexpected thing. He

circled rapidly several times, then quickly dashed in. Before the man was aware of it, the dog seized the stick firmly in his teeth. Gerrit was caught completely by surprise and failed to grasp the weapon firmly. With a twist of his neck, the intelligent animal disarmed his attacker.

Until this time the spectators had more or less enjoyed the struggle between the two. A joking word of encouragement now and then had shown that none of the party took the combat very seriously. But the loss of Gerrit's weapon changed everything. An unarmed man in the presence of an infuriated wolfhound! And his friends could do little to help him before the beast dropped the club and once more began the ferocious attack. The force of the impact threw Gerrit off balance, and he fell in a huddled lump to the ground. Instinctively he hunched himself to protect his throat from the fangs of the dog.

At this critical point, four men of the party leaped the fence and with hastily gathered sticks, beat back the wolfhound. It was only after a merciless punishment of blows and kicks that the dog withdrew a few yards, growling and whining in pain.

Crack! Pssing-ng-ng! The crack of a rifle and the whine of flying lead! The "Man in Bearskin" sat in his tree fondling a smoking gun.

The intruders looked aghast at each other. Gerrit sprang to his feet. The Dominie gasped in breathless excitement.

Crack! Crack! Two shots in rapid succession!

The beast seemed to notice the men's distress; some of them had dropped their clubs. He rushed into the group, growling, barking, snapping.

25

This was no time for a show of bravery. Flight was all-important, and none of the men needed to be told. They turned with one accord and leaped the fence with amazing nimbleness. Once on the other side, they stopped a rod or two within the woods to talk things over. The dog seemed pleased at his victory and paced back and forth just within the enclosure, warning them to be more cautious in trespassing on strange property.

Somewhat ashamed by their speedy retreat, the men talked about the terrible dangers they had faced, to prove that they were not really cowards. One man, nursing a bitten leg and modestly holding together his torn pants, grumbled angrily, "That miserable brute! I wish I had gotten a sound whack at his skull with my club."

"And that crazy fellow with the gun! Why did he shoot at us when we tried to pay him a friendly visit?" asked another, nursing an arm that had been bruised when a friend had accidentally struck him with his club.

"I don't like this at all," said Dominie Van Raalte. "That fellow seems to have weapons stored in that hollow tree, and between him and his dog he can hold out against a whole party of men if it ever becomes necessary to try to capture him. He's safe to go about doing mischief with very little chance of being caught."

Gerrit was puzzled by the behavior of the "Man in Bearskin." True, he had brought the family food when they needed it badly. But the man's violent actions today strengthened Gerrit's belief that underneath the kindness was some deep, hidden desire to do him harm. He was greatly disappointed at not

26

having a chance to meet the strange person face to face. Still, he could somewhat understand the man's actions. He lived alone in an out-of-the-way place and may have been somewhat alarmed at the appearance of a large party of strangers. The fear would have been increased by their attempt to approach his home in spite of the dog's attack. Perhaps he was a squatter without legal right to the land, and he may have thought the party a group of settlers come to take over his property.

Moreover, the shots which he had fired were merely warnings. An average marksman, at so short a range, could easily have hit any member of the party. Yet three shots had been fired without hitting anyone. Evidently, he only wanted the men to go away and leave him alone. He was not trying to injure anyone.

Gerrit shared these thoughts with the other men. They agreed that perhaps they should not have tried to force their way onto someone else's land. Perhaps those living on the frontier thought that to be very rude conduct. At least the party agreed to leave the land in full possession of the "Man in Bearskin" and his faithful hound.

So the dwelling of the mysterious person had been uncovered, and the man himself seen in full daylight. Yet to Gerrit and the party of friends, he was surrounded by still greater mystery, and his real character was a still greater puzzle. To Gerrit, the whole matter had become even more serious, for underneath it all he feared persecution for himself and his family. It was a more thoughtful, concerned, Gerrit Kolf who returned to the village that evening.

3

Four days later, in the morning, the "Man in Bearskin" set out from his hut on the hill to bag a deer. He was dressed as usual in the great hairy cloak with the hoodlike cap. He left his faithful companion at the rail fence.

"Stay here, Wolf," he commanded. "You'll have to watch the place while I'm gone. I'm going out to get a buck, and there'll be a juicy bone for you, if you tend strictly to business. Now get back to the hill, old boy, and I'll be back pretty soon."

The intelligent hound obeyed as if he understood perfectly the command of his master. In another moment the man entered the quiet forest and strode through the giant columns of hemlock and oak.

His bearskin cape, his rugged body, and his lively step made him appear to be a man of great strength and excellent health and energy. Yet, if you looked carefully at his face, you could see that he was not a young man but a man of middle age. Although his face was almost hidden by a great beard, his high forehead, his fine nose, yes, all of his facial features suggested that here was a man of great intelligence, an extraordinary man.

It was his eyes that attracted most attention. They were brownish black, deeply set, and in them was the look of deepest sorrow. Most of the time he gazed down at the ground before his feet as if he cared little for what was about him. The man's whole appearance suggested that he was troubled and unhappy. Something about his look and step also told you that his mind was set on some important business.

He had gone for some distance into the dense woods, and now he began to look for signs of game. He seemed to be somewhat absorbed in other things rather than in the woods immediately around him. At least, he failed to come upon any signs of game. His step slowed down to a mere stroll; he handled his gun absentmindedly.

He continued walking until he arrived at a small elevation in the heart of the forest. A little stream wound around its base. Seeing a fallen log, the hunter sat down to rest. The beauty of the surroundings struck a soft spot in his soul. He loved the tinkling brook, the still air, the woody freshness of the forest. His rifle lay unnoticed at his side, his head drooped to rest upon his hands, his whole posture made it clear that something was indeed troubling the "Man in Bearskin."

He had sat this way for a full half hour when he was roused by the drumming of a flock of grouse. He started as if he had been suddenly brought back from thoughts of faraway times and places. He sighed aloud, picked up his neglected gun, and strode off into the woods.

An obstacle lay across his path. Two fallen trees, gnarled and twisted, entangled through each other, were in his way. There seemed no suitable way around, for the underbrush was closely grown together. The hunter decided to climb over.

The bark of the trees was overgrown with slimy lichens and moss. As the man stretched to his full height to step from one trunk to the other, he slipped, and both feet shot through the narrow slit between the two trees. A sharp, twitching pain ran through his left leg; he struggled to release himself, but it was of no use. He was firmly imprisoned between the two great trees. He was alarmed to discover that his left foot was caught in a viselike angle formed by a hidden branch on the underside of the tree.

He first tried to free himself by lifting his body with the aid of his arms. But the weight of his body and the force of his hard fall had wedged him securely between the trees, and he found it a hopeless task to free himself.

The pain in his foot was almost unbearable. He knew now that the hidden branch had so twisted his foot that his ankle had been severely wrenched and possibly broken. The slightest movement in his struggle to free himself made him wince and groan.

The hunter was well acquainted with the wilderness; he realized the terrible danger he was in. He was a prisoner in the unbreakable grip of the two trees. He shuddered to think that he must remain in the loneliness of the night woods, helpless, unarmed, immovable, to be chilled by the night winds, to be teased by the pangs of hunger, and worst of all, to be tormented by the thirst for water. Besides, it was not at all unlikely that a prowling bear or a hungry wildcat would discover him and make a meal of him.

In his imagination he already felt the gnawing hunger, the burning thirst. He saw his starved body reduced to a mere frame of bones still held in the grip of the great trap. He felt the hot breath of the snuffling bear, the tearing claws of the striking wildcat. The cold, clammy sweat of horror stood out on his face, his breath came in whistles, and in the agony of his terror he could hardly suppress a scream.

The fear which filled him moved him to a second effort at freeing himself. The hopelessness of his situation lent strength to his arms and power to his legs. So intense were his efforts that he barely felt the pain in his injured ankle. But his efforts only exhausted him. The fallen trunks did not budge one inch. He became more certain than ever that he could never free himself.

The thought of death filled him with an unspeakable dread. The fear of the unknown, the terror of meeting an angry God filled his soul. Yet he did not pray.

"No! No! I will not die!" he shrieked in a raging voice. "I cannot die here, alone, in this forest. What will become of my plans? How shall I repay the debt? I must be freed. I—I—I," and he ended in a mumble of angry sobs.

His eyes scanned the surrounding forest as if to command the silent trees to bring him a deliverer. But no sign of life was to be seen. Once more he tried his own strength. Frantically he twisted. He pulled at the bark, squirmed about in his narrow prison, wrenched, and struggled, but it was useless. Again his spirits sank; he relaxed his whole body; his head drooped upon his chest. He was hopelessly doomed to die.

An hour passed, and another. Already it was long past noon. In a little while the comfort of the bright sunlight would change to gloomy darkness. The wolf would leave his den to prowl the woodland. The bear would rise from his warm, sunny bed to set out in search of berries. The tawny cat would slip through the forest on pads of velvet, hungry and merciless. The owl, perched in the treetop, would hoot its weird call to add the the terror of the victim. The forest would be cold and dark, darker than a deep pit.

Forest creatures came to mock him. There, only a few paces from him, stood a timid buck, gazing in bewilderment at the imprisoned hunter. The graceful animal sniffed the air with his dainty nostrils, tossed his wild head toward the soft breeze, grew alarmed at the motions of the hunter, snorted, and turned to the cover of the forest. A little wren chirped with gusto on a limb ten feet above him as if to make him jealous of its freedom. A chattering squirrel leaped on the tree trunk near him, squatted on its haunches, and scolded him. The hunter hated the little beast for mocking him. He felt his hands clench in anger.

What was that? A human voice? He had not thought of human aid. The accident had happened far from the village, out of the lane of travel. The Hollanders hunted near home. There was plenty of wildlife there for their needs. The Indians had moved their village northward for a season. It seemed unlikely that anyone would come to this particular spot where the hunter was in such great need.

But was that a human voice? The "Man in Bearskin" strained his ears to listen. Far off he heard a cry, a cry of someone in need of help. Great joy suddenly filled him. He tossed back his head and shouted. Rescue at last!

"Thank God! I'm saved!" he breathed in delight. But the words were only an expression of his great relief. There was no real thankfulness in them.

Again the cry came through the forest—a long, wailing call of distress.

"Halloo-ooo-ooo! Halloo-ooo-ooo!" The hunter raised his voice in response. To make his voice carry farther, he cupped his hands around his mouth and turned his head in the direction of the welcome cry.

There was no reply except the echo of his own voice. All the joy seeped from him. He was not to be rescued after all? His despair was blacker than it had ever been. But he was certain that he had heard someone. Then he remembered that the call had sounded as if someone was in distress. It was a call for help, like his own. Was it possible that someone else was in great trouble and that the two of them were unable to help each other? What a thought! Two helpless wretches doomed to die in the dark forest, within calling distance of each other, yet too far away to give help or comfort. Was the other person silent now because he had already died? Better to die than to suffer like this!

But the "Man in Bearskin" would not give up hope. With all the might of his powerful lungs he yelled loud and long, "Halloo-oo-oo! Come here! I can't come to you!" Again and again he repeated to call, first in Dutch, then in English, then in Dutch again. Anxiously he waited for a reply. He was excited and tense, hoping against hope for an answer.

And it came! Not a whimper this time, but a firm, clear call. It was nearer than before. "I'm coming," it said, "I'm coming."

Never had the hunter heard a sweeter sound than

these three short syllables. They were surety of hope, the guarantee of life. "I'm coming!" the call came again.

"Here! Here I am," returned the "Man in Bearskin." He eagerly guided the rescuer with the sound of his voice.

The noise of someone approaching reached the imprisoned man. And now that rescue was certain, new worry disturbed him. Would the needed friend recognize him? The language of the caller had been Dutch. Would his rescuer know him and tell everyone who he was? This concern made him draw his great hood and cape tightly about him until only his beard, nose, and a set of brown eyes were visible.

"Where are you?" came the voice from the forest.

"Here! Here I am! I'm caught between two windfalls and can't get out without help."

The tread of feet was now plainly audible, the crackling of twigs, the brushing aside of branches. In an instant the rescuer would stand before him. Who would it be?

Down the stately aisle of the woodland cathedral walked a slender boy. He was dressed in the quaint garb of a Holland immigrant. He wore wooden shoes, thick knitted stockings, baggy woolen trousers, a small, tight-fitting jacket, and a black cap with a large visor. He walked with an air of wonder and hesitation to the place where he saw the trapped hunter.

"A beardless boy!" exclaimed the latter. And then to himself he added, "He, at least, won't know me."

The youngster stood a short way off, not knowing just what to do. It was plain that he was uneasy, and untrained to deal with such emergencies in the wilderness.

"Come and help me," said the hunter, aware of the youth's uncertainty and afraid that he might bolt, like frightened deer, into the neighboring forest. "Come and help me. My body is wedged between these two trees, and my foot is clamped by a heavy branch. I can't move without the most terrible pain. Don't be afraid of me."

The boy, who could not have been more than fourteen, gazed with awe and wonder at the "Man in Bearskin."

"Oh! It's the 'Man in Bearskin'!" he breathed in evident terror. His slim body chilled with fear as he spoke the dreaded phrase, and he turned as if to flee.

"Are you afraid of me, youngster?" asked the anxious hunter, conscious of the critical state of affairs. "Don't fear me; I'll not harm you. How could I hurt you if I wanted to while I'm fast in the grip of these cursed trees? If you can help me out of my predicament, I'll make it worth your while. Come now, be reasonable and give me a hand."

"I don't dare to come near you," said the boy in a doubtful voice, still standing at a safe distance.

"But why? I tell you I'll not harm you. I do harm to no one, least of all to those who help me."

"Aren't you the 'Man in Bearskin'?"

"Yes, I am."

"Then you are the one who has tried to kill our people. You shot at them with that very rifle there. I've heard of you. I don't dare to set you free."

"But my gun lies there on the ground, boy," impatiently said the hunter. "You can get it and do

35

what you want with it. But come, are you going to help me?"

The imprisoned man began to be irritated by all this talk. Why was the boy so disturbed that he hesitated to assist a helpless hunter who needed him so desperately?

The thoughts which ran through the mind of the boy were confused and excited. He had heard the story of the happenings at the shelter of the hunter, he had listened with awe as the men told of the unusual clothing and unexplained actions of the lonely woods-dweller, and he imagined the mysterious person to be more terrifying than the Bluebeards and giants about whom he had read.

Yet the boy was old enough to know that the man was in great danger and in need of help. Moreover, he himself had been seeking help. He had lost himself in the forest and was uneasy at the thought of passing a horrible night in the blackness and wildness of the woods. Perhaps the two could aid each other.

Overcoming his dread, the boy walked toward the helpless hunter. He cautiously neared the fallen rifle and picked it up with respectful care. The hunter was overjoyed at the promising change in the boy's attitude.

"Be careful with the gun," he said. "It's loaded." It was plain from the way the lad acted that he wasn't used to handling firearms. He took it gingerly from the ground, held it far from him, and, at the warning words of the man, laid it carefully aside, leaning it against a nearby beech.

"How can I help you?" he asked.

"I hardly know myself how you can best help me.

36

Perhaps, by adding your strength to mine, I can be lifted out of the crevice. Let's try that first anyway."

The boy, now that he was determined to help, moved quickly and surely, to the surprise of the hunter. He climbed with ease on the fallen trunks, stood astride them, and, somewhat shyly at first, put his slender arms under the shoulders of the entrapped man.

"Now! Let's go together!" said the man.

The boy heaved with all his might; the man strained and lifted and struggled. But the jaws of the great trap held him fast. It was useless to try more.

"This won't do," said the man. "It's that branch underneath that holds me tight. It bites my ankle like a steel beartrap. We'll have to get that foot loose first."

The man did not know exactly how the injured foot was caught. It was underneath the trunks of the trees, and they were too large for him to see around them.

"Can you crawl under and see how my foot is fastened?" he asked. "See if you can find a way to free it."

The youngster acted immediately. Lying low, he crawled under the two fallen trunks. There was not much room to move about, but the boy's body was small and he wormed his way to where the man's ankle was caught. He noticed that the man's foot had slipped into a crotch formed by the trunk of the tree and a stout limb about two inches thick.

"Now, when I pull, you try to work your foot loose," advised the boy from his position under the windfalls.

He pulled and strained in his hampered position in an effort to widen the crotch and so release the foot. The man added his efforts to those of the boy, but the limb was too strong for the boy, especially since he could not, on account of his position, use his full strength. For a moment both were baffled by the failure of the two attempts. The man especially was provoked.

"I have it," the youngster cried. He came crawling out of the small aperture, looked about until he found a short, stout stick, and then returned to his post under the trees. He inserted the stick a short distance above the man's foot. Then he called to the man to try again. The boy used the stick as a lever, applying every ounce of strength he had. The limb yielded a little. The foot moved a fraction of an inch. It was a promising sign.

"A little more," groaned the man in excruciating pain. "It's coming," and he drew his breath with a sharp whistle. The boy outdid himself in a last supreme effort. His slender arms trembled with exertion, his eyes bulged from their sockets, the peak of his strength had been reached. A final wrench, a pull, and the foot was free.

"Oh-h-h!" breathed the hunter in relief and pain. "My foot!"

It took only a moment to finish the task of freeing the man. When he was once more on the ground, his legs crumpled up under him, and he lay in a heap on the black humus of the forest floor. He was free, but at the cost of so much nervous energy and physical strength that he couldn't stand up. The boy was touched by the helplessness of the man who had so recently filled him with fearful imaginations. He felt weak himself and sat down on the root of a tree to calm himself and consider the next step to be taken.

"Can I do anything for you?" he asked with kindly concern. He seemed to have lost all fear of the stranger.

"I'm not sure," replied the freed man, "but I'm afraid my foot is useless. I may need your help to get back to my shelter."

"You surely were in a pretty fix," observed the boy. "You were a good deal like Paul in prison, but you didn't have a jailor to set you free."

"Paul! What Paul do you mean?"

"Why, Paul! Paul of the Bible. The apostle Paul! Didn't you ever hear of him?" The boy was clearly surprised, for his Dutch parents had faithfully taught him the stories of Bible heroes, and he was shocked to think that there could possibly be an adult who did not know about Paul.

"Oh!" exclaimed the hunter in a scornful tone, "*that* Paul."

"Yes, but he was freed in a more wonderful way than you were. Silas was there too, and they prayed to God, and He answered them by setting them free. Did you pray when you were caught?" The boy's open, honest speech and especially his frank question embarrassed the hunter. The boy had been trained in a Christian home where prayer was common, and it was only natural that in times of great danger his first thought would be to pray. But the "Man in Bearskin" clearly was not a godly man, for he made a queer grimace at the boy's remarks and answered only with a mocking laugh.

The night was not far off, and it was important

that the two start for home immediately. The man made an effort to rise, but the jab of pain that ran through his leg threw him back with a grunt.

"I'm going to have a hard time of it getting back," he said, looking ruefully at the injured leg.

"Yes, and I'm anxious to get home myself," the boy said. "I'm lost and can't find my way out of the woods. I thought you might be able to direct me to the colony, but I see that you won't be able to take me there."

"So you're lost, are you? What are you doing in this wilderness, alone and unarmed?"

"It's my own fault," Jacob murmured. "I intended to go only a little way, but I came across a big rabbit and I started to chase him. Before I knew it, I had gone so far I wasn't able to get back. I roamed around until I became so frightened that I thought I better call for help. Then I heard you answer, and I came over here to you." The strangeness of his surroundings and the signs of approaching night combined to upset the courage of the young Hollander, and he wiped the sleeve of his jacket across his eyes to hide his tears.

"My father will be wild with anxiety, if I don't get back tonight. He's warned me time after time to be careful in the forest, and he'll be angry with me, too."

"Your father? Oh, yes! Who is your father?" asked the hunter in an attempt to take the boy's mind away from his present misfortune.

"My father's name is Gerrit Kolf."

The man started as if stung by a wasp. His eyes widened with surprise, his mouth fell open. "Gerrit Kolf!" He spoke the name in an awe-struck voice.

40

"Yes," said the boy, "and my name is Jacob."

"Jacob Kolf! His son! The son of Gerrit Kolf!" The hunter eyed the boy as if he were looking at some freak in a side show—some unnatural creature.

"You seem to know my father," said the boy in a tone of wonder.

"Boy, why do you say that?"

"Well, you gave him a deer at the lake, and a sack of meal the next day."

"But can't one bring gifts to those who are needy without necessarily knowing them personally?"

"Yes, but you knew my father's name; you wrote it on a piece of paper. I saw it myself." The man was silent, not having a reply. "But what is your name, sir?"

"I am the 'Man in Bearskin.'" He uttered the words slowly and solemnly, letting them work their full power on the boy's lively imagination.

"The 'Man in Bearskin,'" repeated the boy in a voice filled with awe. "But you must have another name, too. What is your real name?"

"I believe you and I are going to be good friends, and we had best understand each other from the start. I have told you the only name by which I care to be known. Use that name as you please, but never ask me for another one. Will you do that?"

"Yes, sir," answered the boy.

"Well, Jacob, our time is worth too much to spend it here in idle talk. We must get back to my hut before the blackness of night covers all familiar trails and landmarks. We can still help each other. I'll manage to get you back to the colony after we get to my shelter. Now get me a stout staff from that young oak over there—here's my knife—and I'll try to hop along somehow."

Jacob did as he was asked and soon had a sturdy cane cut from the sapling. The pair set out in the direction of the grassy park, the hunter propped upon his crude crutch, hopping along and accepting the support of Jacob's shoulder. Beside the hunter walked the boy proudly carrying the cripple's rifle. Through the solemn corridors of the forest they walked. The boy talked constantly with the open-heartedness and frankness of his age, but the man heard little of what he said. While Jacob prattled boyishly, the "Man in Bearskin" was seeking a way out of the maze into which his thoughts had led him.

"Jacob Kolf," he thought. "Son of Gerrit! Yes, the boy has his father's features—the same chin, the same eyes. Gerrit must be the same as he used to be, always bringing in God and the Bible and prayer. The boy talks just as his father used to talk. But he was a good Gerrit—better than I. Yes, a thousand times better." He stopped his chain of thought to permit other thoughts—pleasant memories—to fill his mind.

The insistent voice of the child at his side called him back to the present. "Sir," asked the boy, "shall I ask my father to visit you?"

The hunter stopped short in his tracks. The question was entirely unexpected. "But Jacob, why should your father think of such a thing? He doesn't know who I am."

"But father would like to thank you for the gifts you made him."

"Jacob, I want no one to visit me. No, I'll allow no visitors on my ground. I've bought the land; I'm

42

the owner. That plot of land is my little kingdom; I am master there, and no one shall trespass on it." The hunter spoke these words with a grimness and determination that made the boy draw back and lift his face toward the bearded face in a questioning way.

"The people all know that you don't want anyone on your land because you shot at them the other day. My father was there too."

"Was Gerrit—er—your father there?"

If Jacob could have seen the face of his companion, he would have noticed that it was bloodless and pale. "Well," continued the man, "if your father tries to force his way, he must be held back too. I'll keep off all intruders. If they persist, I'll use my powder and lead. But what did your father and the other men want on my property?"

Then Jacob told the full story of the party of land-seekers and their adventure at the enclosure.

"So!" sighed the man in relief. "They were looking for land. And how did they fare?"

"Father said that he would stay in the neighborhood of Holland because he doesn't want to borrow any more money to buy land. He is going to work for the other colonists for a while. We have a little hut of boughs now, and father helps the other men clear the land. Before winter comes we'll build a hut of logs. But now we're too busy for that. Isn't it a strange life around here? But it's fun though," he added, remembering the adventures the family had experienced.

"Do your parents need anything?" asked the "Man in Bearskin" considerately.

"No, sir, not just now. But we are living so differently here. Just imagine! We have no closets, no table, no chairs—nothing that belongs in a home. We use a chest that we brought from the Netherlands as a closet and table at the same time. A few blocks of wood are our chairs and the boughs of cedar and hemlock make up our beds. Some of the people," he continued in an unbroken stream of words, "are dissatisfied and are blaming Dominie Van Raalte for bringing them here. Father says he is a wise and a good man and that he knows what he is doing. I hear that more people are coming here from Zeeland and Friesland. I'm glad that there are more people coming, but some folks are afraid that there won't be enough food for everyone if too many people come. It's strange," continued the boy, changing the subject, "it's strange not to have to go to school. We haven't any church either, except outside in the open air. But the Dominie said that there would be one before winter."

The steady flow of news about the colony had caused the man to forget his painful ankle somewhat, and before he knew it, he found himself at the rail fence surrounding his little cabin. Wolf came rushing out to honor the return of his beloved master. The smart animal seemed to know that his master had met with some misfortune, and he leaped and pranced about him in great joy.

The dog was less friendly to Jacob. He advanced toward him and began to sniff around suspiciously as if to make sure that the boy was friendly and that he could trust him.

"Wolf," said his master, "the boy is my friend, and he must not be harmed. He helped me and saved my life, and we must be good to him. Do you understand?" and he patted the dog gently as if to enforce his words. "Don't be afraid of Wolf, Jacob. He won't touch you against my will. He'll be your friend in a little while now."

Jacob was uneasy at the presence of the great animal whose ferocity had been the subject of so much excited conversation after the return of his father and the party of land-seekers. But the commands of the hunter changed the attitude of the dog so much that Jacob found it hard to believe what the men had said about him.

The injured man was now safely seated on a block of wood in his rude home. Jacob was curious about the interior of the cabin and glanced about with quickly shifting eyes. The shack was not unlike the home from which he himself had started that very morning. A framework of saplings, hastily thrown up and notched together with the additional strength of a few wild vines, had been covered with many hemlock boughs. One end of the frame was left open to serve as a door and window combined. The floor was the damp earth warmed by a covering of pine and hemlock needles. Through the small, irregular openings in the covering could be seen the last dim light of the departing day.

The only furniture in the room was the block of wood on which the owner was sitting. A heap of white ashes near the door indicated the place at which the woodsman prepared his meals, and an iron skillet and a heavy pot set in one corner was the complete kitchen equipment of the modest hut.

"You see, Jacob, that I have few of the home comforts you mentioned on the trail. I can't even offer you a block to sit on, for I never expected to have a visitor. If you are tired you had better sit on the ground."

"Why do you choose to live such a lonely life?" asked the inquisitive youth as he gazed with wonder at the bare interior of the man's home. "Why do you live here, and why won't you let anyone visit you?"

"Such questions you mustn't ask, Jacob. I can't answer them for a very good reason."

"What a strange man!" the boy thought, but he kept his opinion to himself.

"Take this gold coin as a small reward for your trouble and your help," said the man, offering a gold piece.

"No sir, but if you can guide me to my home, you will have paid me for my help. I can't take your money."

"Come on, boy! I want you to take it," said the man as he forcibly thrust the coin into Jacob's hand. Jacob could do nothing but accept it as he stammered his thanks.

The short, northern twilight had deepened into night. The boy was growing more and more uneasy in his desire to return to the village.

"Will you tell me the way home now?"

"Yes, but I must ask of you one more thing. Will you come to visit me once a day for a while to help me with my injured foot? I'll need someone to collect a little wood and haul water from the spring."

"Me?" Jacob exclaimed. "I don't know whether my parents will let me."

The man was uncertain just how to overcome this difficulty. "Tell them," he said, "that I must have help, and I will pay you for your services in gold."

"No," answered the boy, "I don't want money to

help you. I'll gladly do it for nothing. I'll come if my father will give me permission."

"Wolf!" commanded the man suddenly. "This little man wants to go to the colony. He is our friend and needs our help. Take the boy home, and guard him well." The hunter reached for a lantern nearby, lighted it, and hung it from the neck of the great dog. "Now, Jacob, Wolf will guide you home. Just follow him faithfully; he knows the way perfectly."

The dog barked as if to thank his master for the compliment and walked out of the hut, looking back as if to tell Jacob to follow. "I'll be back in the morning," said Jacob as he parted with the hunter and followed his guide.

The "Man in Bearskin" watched the disappearing gleam of the lantern as long as he could. When the tiny light had been swallowed up in the thickness of the night, he continued to stare into the solid darkness outside. He sat, deep in thought.

"What a coincidence," he muttered half aloud, "that it should have been his son. I like the lad for his frankness and helpfulness, but I wish he would keep quiet about that everlasting religion. The very image of his father! And he wants to bring his father here! No! No! That must not happen. He would surely recognize me. I wish that I had that bag once more. What a misfortune! I must get it. I will get it, or something terrible will happen!" His determined words were enforced by a click of his jaw and the clenching of his hands. His eyes burned with fervent heat; the veins of his neck stood out. It was some moments before he could recover control of himself and set about nursing his injured foot.

In the meantime Jacob and the dog were proceeding toward the village. Jacob had never experienced the woods at night after the cheerful light of the sun deserted them. The tall tree trunks were faintly outlined by the flickering light of the lantern, and their shapes stirred up within Jacob images of supernatural beings whose scrawny, naked arms stretched out to draw him like magnets into their grasp. The long, soft howl of a timber wolf far off on a distant knoll froze the blood in his veins and hastened his steps. From a hidden bough near at hand, an owl hooted weirdly. A short way off, possibly on the shore of Black Lake, a loon laughed. It was all so unusual, so new, so strange to the Dutch boy. Yet as he walked along without meeting with any harm, he began to enjoy the thrill of the adventure, to feel proud of his manliness, to sense the throb of a courageous heart.

Jacob was greatly relieved, however, when the lesser darkness of a small clearing appeared before him, and he could make out the hazy outline of a dwelling. The dog stopped without command and seemed to consider his duty done. A closer look at the place assured Jacob that he was familiar with it and that it was unnecessary for the dog to go farther.

"Wolf, you have done well. You had better go back to your master now." But the dog had already turned and was quickly disappearing in the dark.

Jacob borrowed a lantern from the colonist at whose hut he had been left by Wolf, and with little difficulty found the modest home of his parents. He told the story of his adventures at once. His father listened eagerly as he repeated his conversation with the mysterious stranger. He was puzzled when Jacob said that the man seemed to already know something about their family. Jacob also told of the unusual way in which the dog had brought him back safely to the colony.

When Jacob showed the glittering gold piece which the man had forced upon him, his father began to scold him for accepting money in payment for what had been his Christian duty. But he was satisfied when Jacob explained exactly how he had been compelled to accept the coin.

"And now, Father, may I go back tomorrow as I promised?" asked the boy, somewhat doubtful of the answer.

"Yes," his father answered thoughtfully, "you may. The man needs help, and since only you are allowed on his property, you must care for him."

The boy was pleased, for he had already become somewhat attached to his new friend in spite of the secrecy that surrounded him. Jacob lay down on his bed of hemlock boughs, not to sleep, but to think of the happenings of the most adventurous day of his life. He lay down to dream of the great man in the bearskin cape, of the man who would shoot all those who came on his land and who was willing to let him, Jacob, a boy of fourteen, be the only person to visit him. The night seemed all too long to Jacob in his eagerness to go back to the lonely hut on the deserted knoll to learn more about this new friend whose life seemed clouded over by exciting mystery.

4

The next morning Jacob was up with the sun. His father acquainted him with the trail to the woodland enclosure and gave him a start in the right direction. Jacob knew that his new friend would be impatient for the return of his nurse, so he hurried through the forest with such speed that he was entirely out of breath when he arrived at the rail fence. Wolf rushed out to meet the early visitor with a great deal of barking and growling, but as soon as he recognized Jacob, he stopped his fierce antics and greeted the boy with a great show of friendliness.

The duties of the young attendant were few and light. He gathered some brushwood for the fire, got a supply of water in a bark gourd from a spring a few hundred feet away, and performed the other little tasks necessary to the simple life of the injured man. On the first day Jacob scoured the neighboring woods and brought back two strong lengths of birch which the hunter soon made into a set of crutches.

For a week Jacob came regularly to the hut in the forest. In that time the injured ankle had healed enough to enable the man to hobble around and help himself. Therefore, he told his youthful helper that it was no longer necessary for him to come every day, but he would be pleased to have Jacob visit him as often as he could.

Jacob proudly accepted the gold pieces given him for his services and stammered a somewhat uncertain promise to return soon. He had hoped to learn more of the peculiar stranger during his visits, but he was keenly disappointed. He found the man as tight-mouthed as a clam. The hunter answered the boy's many prying questions with short and uninformative replies.

Jacob had been further mystified by the great hollow tree which stood in the rear of the shelter. Once he had ventured to approach it, but the man's watchful eye caught the movement. Jacob was forbidden to go near it. This made Jacob even more curious about the tree, and he imagined within its hollow depths no end of strange, uncommon things. He saw stacks of long rifles, heaps of ammunition, knives, sacks of gold, and stores of treasure. For Jacob was convinced that the man was wealthy. He himself had received generous gifts of precious gold and he was sure that the secretive man of the forest was the possessor of many sacks of gold.

What troubled Jacob most was where the gold came from and why the man lived so poorly, without human friends. For in his brief visits the boy had seen more fully the extreme simplicity of the lifestyle of the hunter and his dog. Their diet consisted entirely of venison and dried bear meat. Even maize, without which the Dutch settlers would have starved, was not part of the menu of the two inhabitants of the shelter. And yet the man had gold enough to buy the choicest food that Allegan and Grand Rapids could provide. Why live in this lonely hut when he could live with other settlers in the cities and share their warm hearth fires, join in their talk and laughter, enjoy an abundance of good food? Could he be a criminal who was fearful of being caught and imprisoned? The man's conduct made Jacob suspect that this might be true, for he had noticed that while alone the man would sit without his great bearskin, but as soon as the boy appeared he would quickly wrap himself up in it. Surely, it seemed as if he must be hiding some dark secret in his heart.

Yet, Jacob could not believe that the man was a robber, for how could he be a thief and at the same time be familiar with his father whom Jacob trusted and respected? This riddle troubled the curious boy, but he continued to serve the hunter, who seemed truly appreciative of his help.

Jacob left the clearing on the last day of his week's service with the hope of some day finding the hunter and his dog away, and then of being able to explore the darksome secrets of the great elm. The dishonor of such sneaky behavior bothered Jacob's Christian conscience somewhat, but his insatiable curiosity and his love of exploration helped to quiet his conscience. Already he found himself anticipating the next visit to the little enclosure.

A few days later the man of the forest left his cabin at midday and limped out into the surrounding woods. It was plain that he didn't intend to be gone long; he didn't take a rifle. Instead he carried a short-handled axe. Coiled on his arm was a length of strong, light rope. From the difficulty with which he walked it appeared that his ankle was not yet completely healed, yet he succeeded in getting along fairly well without crutches.

He had gone only a few hundred yards from the

shack when he came to a stand of maple—small, slender saplings. The denseness of the little grove was broken only by two or three larger trees. This place seemed to be the destination of the hunter's excursion, for he laid down the coil of rope and immediately began to fell the slender trees. In a short time he had collected a considerable pile of saplings.

He was standing motionless for a moment to rest himself when his ear caught the sound of something moving in the bush. Cautiously he picked up his coil of rope and threw it around his body. He could not make out the sound, but he wanted to be prepared to run if necessary.

He stood in an expectant attitude, listening closely to catch some sound that might tell him what creature had alarmed him. It might only be a harmless squirrel, or a fox. There! What was that? A heavy crashing of tender trees as if a great body was making its way through them! A wolf? No! The hungry wolf was too stealthy; it would not have given a warning. The thought of an Indian was equally ridiculous, for the wily men of bronze were as silent as the gliding moon when they moved through the forest.

The sound was repeated, nearer now. The tread of a heavy body over dry twigs, the swaying of the leaves in the tops of the saplings pointed strongly to the presence of a bear. At the thought of meeting such a fierce animal, the hunter shuddered. He clutched the handle of his axe with nervous determination. He thought of his rifle, useless in the cabin.

A low growl not ten paces from him dispelled all doubt. For an instant the hunter was riveted to the spot. In his terror he could think of nothing but the clawing paw and the crushing embrace. Flight? Impossible. How could he with one good leg outrun a bear? That was absurd. Better to stand his ground with a keen axe in his hand than to turn his back to a pursuing beast. Perhaps, after all, the great animal would pass by unsuspecting.

As he looked around for some way to save himself, he noticed a great maple about ten feet behind him. That gave him an idea. His axe would be much more useful in the limbs of that tree than on the ground. Without a second thought, he turned and with all the might of his arms and legs began to climb to the leafy haven. Over his shoulder hung the coil of rope, from his belt protruded the handle of the axe.

The sound of his rapid movements had alarmed the approaching beast. The great black bear shuffled through the thicket and burst into the little opening around the maple. His growlings and his loud "woofs" served to speed the hunter's climb into the protection of the maple.

The animal stopped near the base of the tree and gazed with stupid wonder at the climbing man. The fate of the hunter depended on the mood of the beast which held him captive. The man was aware of this. When he had reached a limb on which he could perch himself, he turned his face to the earth and watched with tense interest the actions of his captor. The bear, in his patient, unhurried way, strolled about the tree, snuffing at its base, occasionally lifting his snout to whiff the air or to stare at the man on the limb above him. The animal seemed in no hurry either to depart or to follow up his advantage. For a time the hunter felt a glowing hope that the fat, furry forest creature would be perfectly content to mind his own business and not concern himself with that of a helpless, unarmed man.

But this hope quickly died. To make climbing easier, the man had cast aside his robe of bearskin. It now lay but a few feet from the inquisitive bear. The animal suddenly discovered the hair hide, approached it cautiously, and examined it closely as if to uncover some treasure of choice food. His disgust at finding it to be but a tough, hairy hide was expressed by a deep, rumbling growl and a change in his attitude toward the man in the tree.

Scorning the cloak made from the hide of his brother, the bear once again approached the tree. In a moment he had begun to climb. The hunter lost no time in continuing his ascent into the upper branches. Perhaps he could perch himself on a limb so small that the climbing bear would distrust it. Fortunately for the man the bear climbed leisurely and with caution.

The hunter realized completely his extreme danger. He knew that his life would be won or lost by a single blow of his axe. He climbed about in an effort to get into a position from which he could best wield his keen-edged weapon. When he had found a place where he could use his right arm freely, he drew his axe from his belt and awaited with pounding heart the on-climbing bear.

The beast was now only six or eight feet below him, and the hunter prepared to deliver the fatal blow. But in that instant something unexpected happened. The man, in order to give the most possible force to his blow, drew his feet up on the limb and clasped with his left hand a smaller branch above. As he was lifting himself into this position a dart of pain shot through his weakened ankle, his foot slipped, and for a second it seemed as if he would be thrown to the ground forty feet below. In a frenzy of fear he clutched at the limb above him with both hands. As he did so, the precious axe fell from his hand. It turned over once in its course before it struck with a soft thud against the upturned nose of the ascending bear. A gruff "woof" of pain arose from the deep throat of the animal. The now useless axe continued its harmless fall to the ground.

The events of the next moment happened with the speed of lightning. The bear, angered at the harmless, yet painful blow on his sensitive nose, lost no time in making for the treed man from whom he knew the blow had come. The man's plight seemed hopeless. A faintness came over him. He sickened to think of his inability to defend himself. His death seemed sure. The last hope had been taken from him. His hands only, poor, weak, fleshy hands, were all he had left. Human hands to wrestle with an enraged bear!

The thought flashed upon him like a puff of powder. There was no time for second thoughts. He crouched on the limb where he stood, looked for an instant at the beast now only a foot or two below him. Then he shot out into the air. He swished with sickening speed through the leafy space below straight for a limb which he had chosen before his leap. It was only ten feet down, but to miss it meant a damaging fall, possibly death. He clutched frantically at the limb with both hands. His fall stopped with a jolt; one hand held uncertainly. In another second he had secured his hold with his other hand, and he swung himself across the friendly limb.

The sudden change in the situation baffled the bear and gave the hunter some time to think. He thought of his faithful dog. He knew that there was a chance of it being within hearing. Perhaps in some way the faithful animal could help him. "Wolf! Wolf!" he called again and again. "Come here!" The sound of his voice informed the bear of what had happened, and the animal looked with his little brown eyes at his victim below.

Slowly the great beast backed down to get to the lower limb on which the man sat. The branch had been severely strained by the force of the hunter's fall. Would man and beast be hurtled together to the ground?

It was then that the man first thought of the rope around his shoulders and of the use to which it might be put. Lifting the coil from his body, and whirling it about his head as freely as he could in his insecure position, he tossed it into the air and over the very same limb from which he had just thrown himself. The aim proved good and the dangling end of the rope swung in to meet him. Grasping the two ropes which now hung side by side from the branch above, the hunter left his perch and climbed with difficulty into the open space between.

The bear had already reached the lower branch and was just venturing out on it when the man left it for the safety of the rope. But the weight of the bear was too great for the cracked limb, and the animal had scarcely gone out on it when it gave way. The frightened beast clawed the air for support, then crashed downward through the foliage. He struck the earth with a heavy thud.

The hunter was delighted. "Now," he thought,

"the brute will have enough. Perhaps he's seriously hurt." With these comforting thoughts he climbed to the limb across which he had flung the rope, believing he was safe now.

But the lower limbs of the maple had broken the fall of the bear and had kept him from serious injury. The man watched with horror as the shaken animal picked himself up, bleeding about the mouth and head, but otherwise unhurt. He was plainly enraged at his fall. To the despair of the hunter, the bear returned to the attack, a more dangerous, determined enemy than ever.

The bear climbed rapidly. He was bleeding, and the taste of his warm blood filled him with a lust for more. He wanted flesh—bloody, juicy flesh, and he fairly ran up the tree to get it.

The rope saved the man a second time. Gathering it in from over the limb, the hunter coiled it quickly, made a noose in one end, and, holding the coil in his left hand and the noose in his right, he awaited the attacker. The animal was now immediately below him. Very carefully the man dropped the noose over the head of the bear and quickly drew it tight about his neck. Swiftly he wound the coil around the limb some five or six feet from the trunk of the tree and let the loose end drop to the ground. Swinging himself over the branch, the hunter grasped the rope, and in a moment slid to the ground.

The bear was puzzled by the tightening noose about his neck. He stopped a moment, trying to remove the bothersome rope. This hesitation had given the hunter enough time to complete his descent. When the bear saw his victim once more escape him, his anger knew no bounds. He turned to climb down the tree. The rope made this impossible and the bear expressed his anger with loud growls and powerful efforts to free himself. The man on the ground, who held the long end of the cord to prevent the rope from slipping, was fearful that the line would snap.

Convinced that he could not get down, the bear began to climb, hoping, it seemed to free himself in that way. As the animal climbed, the hunter pulled hard to take in the slack of the rope. It was in this way that he succeeded in bringing the bear out on the limb from which he could not return. But the now alarmed beast was not to be held without fighting back. When he was certain that it was the thin, white line that held him prisoner, he struggled to pull it apart. He pulled and snapped and growled, trying now this way now that to free his neck from the tightening noose.

The earnest efforts of the entrapped bear made the hunter realize that he could not hope to hold the animal for a long time. So he tied the long end of the rope around the trunk of the tree, and resolved to make his escape. If possible he would get his rifle and return to make an end of the bear.

It was then that the "Man in Bearskin" heard the well-known bark of Wolf, and in a short moment the great dog came bounding through the thicket to the place where his master stood. The hunter was overjoyed at his appearance, for now he felt certain of getting the bear.

"See, Wolf! What is in the tree? That's a bear, old boy, and he's our meat. Watch him, Wolf!"

The dog was quick to discover the treed animal and made a furious show at rushing up the tree and devouring the luckless Bruno. The hound circled the base of the tree at great speed as if waiting for the kill. The hunter cast a mocking glance at the helpless bear and noticed that the demonstration of the dog was not at all to his liking. The bear increased his efforts to release himself; the rope was strained to the breaking point, but it held.

The hunter was just about to hobble his way to the shack, when the thicket opened and the familiar figure of Jacob stepped into the clearing. The boy was breathless from overexertion and could scarcely speak.

"What's the matter?" he asked with deep concern. "I came to your cabin a short time ago, and just as I got there, Wolf pricked up his ears as if he heard something alarming. He kept moaning and whining. All of a sudden he leaped the fence and made off into the woods. I was so surprised I didn't know what to do. I ran all the way and nearly got lost again coming here."

"Jacob, you're just in time. We have a bear treed in that maple," pointing to the animal, "and you can return to the cabin and get my gun. You know where it is. Bring along some extra cartridges. Be careful, son, it's loaded. Now go, and hurry."

Jacob looked in amazement at the hairy, black beast in the tree, the first bear he had ever seen, and his excitement was so intense that he paid no attention to what the hunter said.

"A bear!" he breathed in awe. "A real, live bear!" When the hunter repeated his command, Jacob turned and scurried into the forest as if both the bear and the hound were snapping at his heels.

"Well, well," chuckled the man, pleased at the

fortunate turn of affairs. "I guess you'll make bear steak for my dinner, old boy, instead of my filling your belly with food. But hold on a minute. I had better get back into my bearskin before I relieve you of yours. Jacob must not see me again without my disguise." He picked up the hairy skin, somewhat dirtied by the trampling of the bear but still in good condition.

Jacob, spurred on by being an actor in a thrilling scene, ran at full speed to the dwelling of the hunter. He found the rifle and cartridges and immediately returned, breathless, wild-eyed, shaking from exertion. The "Man in Bearskin" took the gun, fondled it with glee, and examined it carefully.

It took only a moment to find a favorable position, draw a bead, and drill the bear with the speeding bullet. The short range, the stationary target, the calmness of the aim made the first shot fatal.

The bear received the lead with a great deal of displeasure. A fierce grunt announced the effect of the shot, a desperate writhing and struggling followed. For a time it seemed as if the rope or the limb must break under the strain, but they both held fast. The struggles of the bear became weaker, the grunts less frequent. Finally his body sank into a heap, he clawed for footing, lost his balance, and fell from the limb. The fierce brute that had so recently threatened a human life now dangled by his neck from the limb, a pendulum of dead flesh.

The hunter watched the proceedings with grim good humor. When the bear had fallen from his perch, he undid the rope and, by shaking it vigorously, so loosened the hitch that held it so that the carcass descended very gradually to the ground. Wolf was especially active and noisy, rushing at the carcass and snapping viciously at it.

The noose was taken from the bear's neck; the hunter began the work of skinning and dividing the body. Jacob was all eyes, for he had never seen this operation before. The deft skill of the hunter proved that he had done the work often, and in a short time the naked body of the bear lay before him. The choicest parts were cut out, wrapped in the freshly removed skin, and carried to the hunter's cabin.

It was a curious little group that filed its way through the forest toward home. Wolf led the way with the eagerness of a healthy animal, sniffing, smelling, running, and circling about, examining every root, barking at every squirrel. Jacob, carrying the rifle and the axe, walked proudly next, turning often to look at the bundle of bear meat on the broad back of the man who brought up the rear.

"How did the bear get into such a funny position?" Jacob asked when the party had arrived at the shack. And the man, as he prepared the meat for drying and the skin for preservation, told the boy of his adventure and how he had managed to escape.

Jacob listened with eager attention. When the story was told, he sat in awed silence for a moment and then said very simply, "Wasn't that a narrow escape though? It was very good of God to save your life like that."

The face of the hunter showed his displeasure. "God!" he muttered. "There it comes again! Always God! That's Gerrit all over."

"Well, Son," he continued as if to dismiss an unpleasant thought, "it was lucky that you appeared when you did. I'm glad you didn't forget me as soon as I no longer needed you. But you surely must come here tomorrow and we'll have a good feast of tender bear steaks. Will you come?"

Jacob thought a moment and then replied, "I'm afraid not—because, you know, tomorrow's Sunday."

"Certainly, Son, that makes it just fine. You won't have to work and you'll have plenty of time."

"But church!" exclaimed the boy. "We have to go to church."

It was clear that Jacob's parents had taught him to keep the Sabbath. All of the settlers in the Holland colony considered Sunday a precious, holy day.

"Where do you go to church?" he asked suddenly, remembering how far the man lived from the colony.

His answer was a mocking laugh. "I never go to church." The bitterness in his voice shocked the boy.

"Do you have a Bible?" he asked wonderingly.

The man was silent for a while, then thoughtfully answered, "Jacob if we are going to be friends, it's best that you don't ask me any questions about church or religion." After a pause he added, "Well, then, you had better come Monday, and we'll have our bear meat then. What do you say?"

"All right, I think my father will let me."

It was now time for Jacob to return to the village. As he left the enclosure, he was greatly puzzled by this man who mocked God, who never went to church, and who refused to answer questions on religion—a topic that was a part of the everyday conversation of Jacob's parents and their neighbors.

The "Man in Bearskin" sat in his tent and watched the receding figure of his little friend. "Religion! Religion! His father was always harping on it, and

63

the child is going the same way. Religion! Church! the Bible!" But after a little while in which he sat perfectly still, he added softly, "I wonder if there is something in it." He sat for a long time thinking, and he said not a word.

5

It was plain from the care which the "Man in Bearskin" exercised as he prepared the meal on the following Monday morning that he intended to favor his young guest with a mouth-watering dinner. The man had built a great wood fire and had let it burn down to a thick bed of glowing coals; he had mixed a batch of dough, kneaded it, and baked it in one of his iron pots. The bear meat had been cut into steaks to be broiled when Jacob arrived.

Wolf was interested in his master's activity. He prowled about, nosed the kettle, and eyed the juicy slabs of meat. The hunter laughed to himself at the antics of his pet and spoke aloud to the faithful beast as to a friend, as people who live alone often do.

"Ja, ja, Wolf! We're busy today, aren't we? It's a sort of feast day. Holidays are necessary once in a while. Usually we have a sober time of it out here. I never thought we'd be here so long when we started out to search for my little sack." His voice became more wistful; he stopped in his work. "And I have not found it yet. I wonder—I wonder how long it will last. I can't understand how it's possible that it should escape me so. I was so certain of the tree! And to make sure, I dug beneath all the other trees around it, but it wasn't there! It must be here! It must be!" He was talking desperately. "Where else

65

could it be? I put it there myself, and no one is here to steal it. I'll find it, I'll find it, if it takes all winter. I must get it, I must! But what if I don't? His face became clouded as a stream of unpleasant thoughts passed through his mind. "I will! I will find it!"

The dog did not understand the words of his disturbed master, but he seemed to know that his friend was troubled, for he crept over to a corner and crouched down in silence beside him. The man shook off his worries and again busied himself with the meal. He began to glance impatiently in the direction from which he expected his young friend to appear. Wolf's joyous bark first announced Jacob's approach. In a little while the boy arrived at the clearing and entered the primitive dwelling.

"Here comes the little fellow at last," exclaimed the hunter. "The feast is spread and waiting for the guest of honor." In a few minutes the and boy was settled eating his first meal of bear meat. He ate with zest, smacking his lips in great satisfaction at the flavor of the well-broiled steaks. When he came to bite into a chunk of the home-baked bread, he was greatly surprised to find it well soaked with delicious honey, and he gulped it down with all the enthusiasm of a healthy boy.

"Umm! Honey!" he exclaimed. "Where do you get this?"

The hunter told him of the swarms of wild bees that flew about the country and stored their treasure in the hollow trees of the forest.

"I must find a nest and get some honey for my father and mother," Jacob said. "The folks are getting sick of the coarse bread we're eating, and a little honey will help a lot to make the meals more pleasant."

"I have quite a supply of it, and I'll give you some," said the man, "and you must take some bear meat along too." Jacob was plainly pleased at this offer.

"How are affairs in the colony?" asked the "Man in Bearskin" in a tone of interest.

"Good," said Jacob. "We're getting bigger all the time. A large group of Frisians arrived lately, and they brought a preacher with them too. His name is Dominie Ypma. They're living in the new shelter we built, but the people from Zeeland are coming soon, and the Frisians will have to make room for them. I don't know where they will go. They say they don't want to stay in Holland because they want clay soil. Just as soon as they find the kind of soil they want, they'll move out, I suppose."

"Huh!" said the man, "there's plenty of clay ground to be found to the east. Let them look around a bit."

"Oh! I guess they'll get settled finally, but it's a hard life for our people to break into just the same," added the boy.

"How do you mean?"

"Well, sir, things seem to be getting worse and worse. The money which the settlers brought with them is nearly gone, and there is no chance for getting more. Then the food supply is always so uncertain, and we can't expect a crop for some time yet. The trees seem endless; we cut hundreds of them down, but there always seem to be more. Some people are beginning to talk of sending their sons and daughters to Grand Rapids and Allegan and Kalamazoo to work as servants and hired men to help out their parents. Dominie Van Raalte said this would be a good thing, and my father talks of sending me to Kalamazoo. I suppose I must go if it's necessary, but I'm not very eager to be hired out to strangers. I'd much rather stay in Holland and chop trees and eat coarse bread."

The unhappy expression on Jacob's face showed plainly that he dreaded the thought of being separated from his family. The man felt sincere pity for the boy and said kindly, "Cheer up, Jacob. You mustn't leave home at all. If bad comes to worse, I'll hire you to come out here and visit me. I'll do it anyway! You come out here every so often, and I'll pay you for it. Surely your father will not object to that."

The boy hardly knew how to take the strange offer, but the light that sprang up in his eyes showed that the idea pleased him.

"I hope that some day you will know why I lead such a secretive life in this lonely place. Some day you will know that your neighbors' suspicions about me are entirely untrue. Do you think that I am a dangerous man, perhaps a thief?" The man earnestly peered into Jacob's face with a look of sorrow and that moved the boy to reply with an emphatic, "No!"

The answer seemed to satisfy the man, for he sat in thoughtful silence for a full moment, and a smile passed over his face. "I'm glad," he said, "that someone has faith in me." But he added nothing more to enlighten the bewildered mind of Jacob. Rather he increased boy's wonder by covering himself more completely with the great bearskin cape.

"Does your father intend to build a log cabin for

the winter?" he asked, changing the subject. "If he doesn't, you had better tell him to prepare a warmer home than he has now, or you folks will freeze next winter."

"Yes, sir, Father has thought of it, but he says there's no hurry. He's working hard for other people in order to earn a little extra money. But you, what are you going to do in winter? You can't live in this shelter, can you?"

"No, if I must stay here next winter, I'll have to put up a log hut." The tone in which this was said suggested the man had intended to say more but decided not to.

"Aren't you sure you will stay here next winter? Where will you go?"

The man ignored the question as if Jacob had not spoken.

"Why did your father come to America, Jacob? Or don't you know?"

"Yes, I know very well," came the answer. "Father saw that in the Netherlands there was no chance for him to provide for us. He could make next to nothing at his work and the family needed good food and clothing. We surely would have been in trouble if Mother hadn't inherited a little money. When Father heard that some Hollanders had settled in America, and that there were opportunities for the poor man, and that everyone could worship God freely here, he decided to move to this country. Several other families decided to come too. We used the little inheritance to pay for our passage. When we got here, we found it very different from what we had expected, and Mother wants very much to return to the old country. But Father is determined to stay. He says that the chances for the future are good, that God will look out for us. There are many others in the colony who are dissatisfied and who are always grumbling that they have been deceived by Dominie Van Raalte."

"Such people judge too quickly," remarked the "Man in Bearskin." "The country around here has great possibilities, but the settlers must undergo a year or two of suffering to become established. Things cannot improve until they have cleared sufficient ground and harvested a good crop."

"That's what Father says," continued Jacob, "But it bothers him that the work should be so heavy. He becomes so tired sometimes that he can hardly drag himself around. It's too bad that he has to work so hard, especially since he could have enjoyed an easier life. My father could have been well off, but his brother, who was two years older, cheated him and made off with ten thousand gulden. The thief left for some foreign land and has never been heard of since. That was my Uncle Dirk. Mother has told me this; Father never speaks of it. But if he had this money, he would have been spared the killing work; maybe we would never have come here. My Uncle Dirk was a rascal though, don't you think so?"

"Yes, Jacob, he *was* a rascal."

Jacob did not notice the emphasis on the word "was." "It was about six years ago that it happened," he continued. "I was only little and don't remember much about it. I do remember, though, how hard my father took it. My mother has told me too how he was awake night after night. He couldn't sleep, he didn't eat, and he hardly talked to anyone. Sometimes my mother thought he'd go crazy, but

70

finally he seemed to get over the blow. He never tried to get the money back or punish his brother. Once I heard him say to Mother, 'Why did Dirk do such a thing? I still can't understand it. But I've forgiven him, and I pray that God has forgiven him too.' Even now Father seems to have times when he's down and hardly speaks. Mother says it's because he loves Dirk so much and is so disappointed that he turned out to be a thief. If Father knew where his brother is living, I'm sure he'd write him and tell him that he's forgiven. Even if he's spent all the money, Father would just be happy to see him again. But I guess we'll never hear from him."

Jacob was surprised to see the effect his story had on his listener. The man seemed upset and was making a great effort to hide his feelings.

"Go on and eat, Jacob," he said as he left the table. "I'll be back in a few minutes." The boy watched as he left the shack and disappeared behind the great elm tree. Wolf followed his master. Had the dog been able to speak, he might have told Jacob of the great struggle he witnessed there. Why was his master so sad, so thoughtful, so terribly disturbed? When the man had gained control of his feelings, he returned to his young guest.

"Well, Jacob, have you enjoyed our little banquet?" asked the hunter.

"Yes, sir," answered the boy, looking up. "But what is the matter with you?" he asked, observing the unusual expression on the man's face. "Are you sick?"

"Not really," was the answer. "I just can't eat any more, but if you're still hungry, go on eating. I'll enjoy watching you."

Jacob seemed satisfied with the explanation and picked up a fresh steak of bear meat. Scarcely had he taken a bite when Wolf rushed from his place in the corner into the clearing, barking furiously.

"There's someone in the neighborhood," said the "Man in Bearskin."

In another moment a man appeared at the edge of the forest and stood at the rail fence.

"A redskin," said the hunter. It was so. There stood an Indian. He was not the noble Indian so often seen in portraits, the Indian whose naked body, adorned with scalp-lock and eagle's feathers, spoke of strength and splendor. Instead, he was a squalid, dirty, lazy Indian—the Indian of the town and reservation after the white man had robbed him of his land and his pride. He was dressed in dirty, ragged trousers and shirt. His left foot was bound in a bundle of filthy rags, his right boasted a torn moccasin. His long, black hair hung in disorder over his shoulders forming a greasy frame about his ugly face. He remained standing at the fence, surveying with curious eye the scene in the little hut before him.

"What does he want?" asked Jacob.

"He is probably a beggar."

"Maybe it's the same one who has been hanging around the colony making a nuisance of himself," volunteered Jacob.

"There are many of them around. The missionaries and government agents have helped some of them to become respectable people, but many others who pass for Christians now are as devilish and tricky underneath as ever before. They often go about Grand Rapids and Kalamazoo begging for money."

"One came to our cabin the other day," said Jacob. "My mother was home alone with the baby, little Hendrik. She was very much frightened by the boldness of the Indian. He threatened to kill the baby if Mother didn't give him money. To get rid of him she gave him a small coin. Maybe this is the same fellow."

"Look, Jacob, and you'll see some fun. He's climbing the fence."

The Indian was actually trying to mount the railing. As soon as he placed one leg over, Wolf snapped at him and bit him soundly in the leg. The intruder drew back with a guttural oath, nursing a bleeding wound in the calf of his leg.

"He'll try to talk to us now," said the hunter, calling Jacob's attention to the gestures of the Indian. "He doesn't want food, but money. He sees no use in hunting his own food. He'd rather buy it with the money given him by some poor soul who has to work for it. If he would take food, I'd gladly give him some. Let's try him once!"

The hunter shook his head "no" to inform the beggar that he had nothing for him, but the Indian was not to be gotten rid of so easily. He remained immovable, persisting in making known his wants by the language of signs. When the hunter vigorously commanded him to move on, he ignored the command with a sneer.

"Here, Jacob, bring him a piece of meat and see if that will satisfy him."

Jacob was taken by surprise. He felt a thrill of excitement at the thought of coming into such close contact with the redskin. He hesitated only for a moment. Taking the slab of appetizing meat, he brought it to the beggar at the railing. To his great relief, the Indian took it with eagerness, muttering, in a jargon unknown to Jacob, a string of deep-voiced syllables, gesturing rapidly, trying to impress upon Jacob that he would rather have money.

The "Man in Bearskin" watched the proceedings from his station in the shack. When he was certain that the Indian was still insisting upon money, he resolved to close the matter once for all. He reached for his gun and appeared to make preparations to use it.

But the Indian was not as stupid as he looked. His alert, roving eye caught sight of the hunter's gun. Quickly, he turned and made for the forest, cursing and pulling ugly faces as he went. Jacob saw the Indian stuff the piece of meat into the pocket of his filthy trousers. There seemed to be no room in the pocket, and as if to make room, the Indian pulled out something and hurled it from him. In a little while he was lost from sight among the trees.

The boy was curious to know what the beggar had taken from his pocket, and he leaped the fence to find out. His astonishment was great when he found it to be only a crumpled piece of paper. He opened it to see if there was anything inside.

"What on earth would a beggar like that do with a piece of dirty paper in his pocket? He surely can't read. This is English, too."

"What have you there, Jacob?" asked the hunter from the cabin.

"A piece of soiled paper," Jacob replied. "He took it from his pocket and threw it away. It doesn't amount to anything."

"Let me see it!"

Jacob handed the paper to him. Instantly, the

hunter's whole body tensed with excitement and anger. His face paled like the grey of wood ash, and he seemed to gasp for breath.

"Did he have this in his pocket?" he thundered. "Did you see right?"

"Yes, sir. I saw him take it out." How could the man be so deeply moved by the sight of the paper? What did he see that Jacob had not seen?

"The scoundrel! Red knave!" the hunter cried in anger. "Where is my gun?" he asked, forgetting in his excitement that he held it in his hand. "Oh! I have it! He can't be far. He's a dead Indian!" He rushed from the hut as rapidly as his injured leg would permit.

Jacob had not the slightest inkling of what it was all about, yet he sensed that something awful had been revealed by the paper, that something worse would happen if the hapless Indian were overtaken by his pursuer. There was nothing the boy could do, so he sat down with Wolf and tried, in his boyish way, to connect the events of the last few hours.

"This is a strange ending to our feast," he thought, as he sat staring at the dense forest into which the man had disappeared. For an hour he sat patiently awaiting the return of his host. He listened intently for the sound of a shot and was glad that he heard none, for he hoped that the Indian might escape with his life. No amount of imagining could give Jacob a hint as to what was going on, and he found himself more puzzled about his new friend than he had evern been before.

Wolf first announced the approach of the returning hunter. He went out to meet his master, but received a harsh word instead of the usual kindly greeting. The face of the man was a picture of mingled rage and disappointment.

"Jacob, you had better go home," he said curtly.

"Did you find him?" the boy asked.

"No!" came the explosive answer. "The rascal had too great a start. But he has not gotten away from me yet. I'll go after him again. I'll follow him until I get him if I have to walk every square foot of wilderness in Michigan."

"Did he wrong you somehow?" Jacob asked.

"Do you think I would be so eager to catch him if he'd done me a favor? Boy, don't ask so many questions."

Jacob saw that it was best for him to leave. He quickly made his few preparations, and with a meek good-by left the cabin.

"Wait a minute, son," said the hunter, softening a bit. "Take this meat for your father. And maybe you'd better not come around again until I let you hear from me. Wolf will bring you a message."

Jacob trudged through the woods to the settlement in a state of wonder and uncertainty. He could not understand man's action. He was sure that the hunter was his very best friend, but he was equally sure that the threats toward the Indian showed a meaner, harder nature. Or did the man have a good reason for being so angry with the Indian?

6

August passed quickly, and the bright skies of September filled the woodlands with their dancing light. It was tragic that there should be so great a contrast in the glorious weather and the gloomy state of affairs in the little settlement.

Jacob had been extremely impatient during the few days following the episode of the beggar, and he decided to visit the woodman's hut without an invitation. When he arrived he found Wolf there alone, and though he waited until nearly dusk, no hunter returned to greet him.

During the following weeks Jacob often went to the little enclosure, but each time he was disappointed in not finding the owner at home. Finally he decided that the hunter spent his days and possibly his nights in search of the elusive Indian and that it was useless for him to try to see the man unless he stayed in the woods after dark. This he did not dare to do.

The colony had grown during the summer months to more than a thousand settlers, including those who lived in the surrounding country. Companies of immigrants had come regularly bringing with them their "dominies," organizing themselves into congregations and settling in or around the original colony at the head of Black Lake.

In June about fifty Frisians had come with Dominie Martin Ypma and settled upon a tract of clay soil twelve miles east of Holland; they called their village Friesland. At various times, the Zeelanders arrived, and under the leadership of Jannes Van der Luyster established themselves at Zeeland, six miles east of Holland. Also a company led by Jan Rabbers came from Groningen and settled three miles to the east of Holland.

In the original colony, the inhabitants had cleared a few trails and roads, and had constructed one corduroy road over a cedar swamp through which it was necessary for them to pass on their way to the still incomplete log church.

To this place the settlers thronged every Sunday. Dominie Van Raalte, preaching fearlessly and forcefully, instilled new hope, new courage, new cheer in the failing hearts, and managed by the force of his own example to spur on the immigrants in the struggle which for a time seemed to have no outcome but defeat.

Gerrit Kolf had been among the most industrious. He had worked ceaselessly for himself and others and had been able to provide fairly well for his family. Acting on advice of the "Man in Bearskin" he had made work of building a winter dwelling for his family and now was the proud of a owner small, though cozy, one-room log cabin.

The work of building the new home had taken just a week. With the help of Jacob and a neighbor, Gerrit had felled and trimmed a sufficient number of logs and dragged them to the building site. The four walls had been formed by simply piling the logs on top of one another, and they had been made tight

78

by stuffing the cracks with a mixture of grass and mud. The builders had cut a door and two windows in the walls, but there was no glass to fill the holes. A square piece of cloth was fitted above to be rolled down during cold weather, and a rough door was hung on two leather hinges. The roof presented a problem. Some of the settlers had used slabs of hemlock bark, but the sun had curled them, so they no longer kept out the rain. Gerrit wanted better material for his roof. Fortunately, a load of lumber arrived just then from Saugatuck, and he bought some thin planks. With the help of these and bark slabs, he succeeded in making a roof that could withstand heavy rains.

To the immigrant family, this new house seemed like a palace in comparison with their temporary shelter. Yet the furnishings and interior were of the barest sort. The floor was the solid hardened earth. The fireplace was poorly built; the smoke often escaped through the cracks around the eaves rather than through the hole which was made for that purpose. There were no beds, simply a neatly piled heap of moss and hemlock needles to soften the ground. A large box served as a table, and three or four sections of a tree trunk took the place of chairs. There was no mirror, no clock, no stove, no dresser—only the absolute essentials.

The settlers also lacked proper clothing. They had brought good woolen clothes with them from the Netherlands. But these had had hard use, and when they began to wear out, there was the problem of replacing them. The settlers didn't have enough money to buy new clothes, and by the beginning of

79

winter, just when they needed warm, sturdy clothing, theirs were thin and threadbare.

Children were outfitted with hand-me-downs from parents. Mothers had to think of clever ways to remake clothing for their little ones. Woolen stockings once worn by father and mother were unraveled and knitted into thick, warm stockings for the youngsters; mother's ample petticoats and father's flowing breeches were remodeled to fit the children.

It was during the autumn months that the grey ghost of disease stalked among the huts of the colony. It came as a breath of wind, silent and unseen. Its phantom form flitted from door to door, touching father, mother, baby with the hand of death. To some it brought fever, to some dysentery; to others it brought smallpox. Swift and sure it was, spreading its poison into every lowly home, attacking both the weak and the strong.

It was no wonder that the disease was soon out of control. There had been much rain; the lowlands were swampy; the houses were chilly and damp. The food was coarse and plain; there was not enough variety for good nourishment. Medicines were scarce, and there were no trained nurses. The drinking water was often polluted.

These were times that tried men's faith in God. Every home had its groaning sufferer, its feverish patient, watched over by an anxious parent or by a child. Strange, homemade medicines and "cures" often only made the sickness worse. Death was so common that people seemed almost hardened to it. Men seemed no longer to care who died and who lived. It appeared that sooner or later everyone would become a victim of the plague. They were sure that this was the end of their colony; the condition seemed hopeless.

There was a man in the settlement who kept his courage. It was Dominie Van Raalte. He was grieved to see his faithful followers so fearfully plagued, but he could not sit by and submit. He must fight the curse with all his strength. He went about from hovel to hovel cheering the mourners, comforting the dying, soothing, helping, praying. In every hut he shed a light of hope, in every heart he kindled a spark of resolution. When the cowardly whimpered, he encouraged them; when the well became sick, he visited them; when the sick died, he buried them. His body seemed tireless. He slept little, but he prayed constantly, fully trusting that God would hear him.

He sent to the city for doctors, for medicines, and for other help. He was only part successful. The doctors who first came were quacks and swindlers who prescribed worthless medicines and made the stricken families pay them their last few coins. Finally a skilled physician came to help him. Van Raalte and the doctor cared for the worst cases, and gave advice and medicine to the nurses of those who were in less need.

So many people died that for a time the dead could not be properly buried. Coffins could not be made, and the stiff forms were laid away under trees, wrapped in a single blanket. There were no formal funerals to honor the dead. A simple prayer, a psalm sung in tearful voices by a handful of mourners, a lowering away into the shallow slit of earth and an undisturbed sleep in an unmarked grave!

The home of Gerrit Kolf was not free from the

presence of the gaunt, gray spirit. It touched the healthy cheeks of Jacob, and they became flushed with fever. It stroked his forehead, and it became dry and hot. It waved its hand over his body, and his strength left him. He took to his bed of moss, and the struggle for life began.

It would have been much easier to win if there had been medicine, for Jacob was a wiry child, hardened by the rough outdoor life. But he became ill before the doctor arrived in the colony, and there was no help. The fever gained in height, and in two days Jacob was a wild-eyed, delirious sufferer among the hundreds of others who were stricken. He lost all desire for food, but his longing for water grew proportionately. He rolled and tossed endlessly, slept feverishly, talked incoherently. Sometimes he would talk of his youngest days in the Netherlands, then of the ocean voyage, of the woods, and of bears and rifles and bear meat.

There came a quack doctor with a quack remedy. Gerrit paid five dollars for a small bottle of it and watched with eagerness the effect of it on his son. But there was no apparent improvement. Each morning and evening the little family—father, mother, and three small children—kneeled reverently on the earthen floor, while the father lifted his prayer to heaven, asking for God's help and God's mercy.

It was a terrible time for the family. To lose Jacob, the oldest child, his father's helper, would have been a terrible blow. Gerrit worried about the danger which the rest of the family ran, now that there was a serious illness among them. What if the mother should become ill and die? Who would care for the

little children? Worse yet, what if he himself should die and leave his family alone in the cruel-hearted wilderness? Gerrit knew it was not right to worry about these things, but still, the worry was always there. It had happened and was now happening to other families. Only today he had seen the shrouded corpse of a father carried to the neighboring forest to be laid away among the silent oaks, while in a little hut a pale wife and two little daughters wept. It was hard, it was sad, but it was true. And he was no better than the dead. It could just as well have been his stiff form that filled the shallow grave under the shadow of the oak.

It was these fears that made Gerrit begin to regret that he had taken his family to this lonely village. Until now he had been cheerful and optimistic, but now he felt his high hopes wane. Vrouw Kolf helped much to increase his feelings of guilt and sorrow. She freely stated her unhappiness with the whole project and said she was sorry she had ever agreed to leave their Fatherland.

In the moments of prayer during which Gerrit opened his heart to God and spoke to Him about his worries and concerns, he felt the supporting care of his Heavenly Father. He knew at these times that it was good for him to be where he was, for Jacob to be sick, for the hardships to be many. In these moments he found the strength and encouragement that helped him endure.

In spite of the lack of medicine, Jacob fought the disease stubbornly and successfully. The crisis passed and the weakened child began to improve. For several days he seemed to gain little strength, and his

parents feared a relapse. Finally, the boy began to eat and to grow stronger; recovery was certain.

During these days Gerrit found it difficult to provide food for his family. He went out to hunt several times, but seemed to have no good fortune whatsoever. Each time he came home without game. Finally his patience was rewarded, and a splendid buck fell victim to his rifle. This was indeed a blessing, for there was hardly a bite of nourishing food left in the cabin with which to feed the hungry mouths. But though his success brought joy to the family for a little while, that joy soon turned to sorrow.

Grietje, the second child, became ill, evidently from the same ailment which had stricken Jacob. The next day Vrouw Kolk was ill and went to bed, and a day after that the remaining two children, both very small, became sick. Wife and three children lying helpless on the moss bed held in the clutches of the fearful plague! And only a half-sick boy to help him! Gerrit felt depressed, and though he said nothing, his face showed a new, deeper bitterness in his soul. To add to his misery, he began to feel ill himself. He dared not say so to Jacob, but the boy noticed it and asked him anxiously if he was sick.

"I don't know, son," Gerrit had said. "It seems as if the very worst is going to happen after all."

"I believe the fever has attacked you too, Father."

The father had turned away to hide his flushed face, for he dared not deny the truth of the boy's statement. As if to drive off the symptoms of illness which Gerrit knew were present, he set himself to accomplish the many duties which now were his. An hour later he came in from outdoors, pale and

tired, with a haggard, driven look in his eyes. He turned to Jacob who was trying to attend to the wants of his little sister and could not suppress a groan.

"Jacob, my boy, it has come. I can't, I can't withstand it. I'm sick, deathly sick, and I must lie down."

Jacob turned to his father with blanched face and tearful eyes. He felt the newly returned strength seep from his body, and a wave of faintness swept over him. He recovered in a moment, but his voice was almost a whisper as he answered, "Don't worry, Father. I'll do what I can. I'm strong now, and God will help me."

"Don't, Jacob, don't exhaust yourself from the very start. I'll get you a pail of water, and if you can manage to give the fevered lips a little drink once in a while, you will have done your duty. None of us will care for food. Keep yourself as well as you can, and trust in God for the rest."

Then Gerrit lay down on the moss beside his wife and children to take his turn in the struggle with the invisible but terrible enemy. He lay down with a heavy sigh, a sigh of weariness, of despair—a sigh that spoke of a father's care and a father's dread. Before he rose again, the sun of many days had tinged the leaves of the forest, the stars of many nights had blinked above the little hut. Before he rose again, Death had twice entered through the crude cabin door.

But the days were longest for Jacob, the nurse of the whole family. The passing hours meant nothing to those who were sick. Their fevered minds were filled with wild dreams; their hot bodies tossed and rolled restlessly; their parched lips knew no sound but "Water!" To them the long night meant nothing but fleeting nightmares of frightening forms, but to Jacob each night was an eternity. He heard the moans; he watched the writhing bodies; he felt the dry lips and burning foreheads. On him lay the burden of relieving their distress, of soothing and caring. Sleep was unthinkable. Food was distasteful. The lonesomeness was unbearable! The long, slow hours of the night passed like the heavy grinding of a great machine, barely moving. If he could only talk to someone or hear an encouraging word from his father or mother. But their lips moved only to mumble sounds he could not understand, their vacant eyes looked only to plead for water.

It was natural that Jacob should begin to feel the effects of his trying vigil. He had barely recovered from the sickness himself. His body was still weak and his spirits were low. The strain of his duties gave him a gaunt, ghostly look. His cheeks became sunken and hollowed.

He had tried to be faithful to his task, but on the third night after his father became ill, he knew that he must permit himself a good sleep. He did not want to sleep. Once before he had guiltily slept for three hours. The restlessness of his charges, their increased moanings, and their pitiful pleadings for water had shamed him greatly, and he had promised himself never to let it happen again. But tonight it was different. The evening had passed in most wretched loneliness; the sufferers had been more quiet than usual. Finally, drowsiness overcame him. His eyes closed, his head drooped, he slipped from the log seat to the floor and sank into a deep sleep.

It was sad—this little drama in the Michigan

woods. A small, dark hut in the forest, shrouded in the dense black of a woodland night, brought into indistinct outline by the blinking light of the fall stars. A fearful stillness in the virgin wilderness—a stillness made more awful by the slight noises in the treetops, by the sighing of the wind. A square, unlighted room, bare, cold, dark; five shadowy forms, prone, helpless, suffering from fever and thirst, moaning softly, sometimes very still. And separate from the rest, in the center of the hut, on the hard ground, a sleeping boy.

While the boy slept he dreamed. He was no longer in the rude cabin with the sick, but in a green park filled with brilliant sunshine. The trees were tall and broad, heavy with deep-colored foliage. The pathways were winding and narrow, leading through beds of fragrant jonquils and gorgeous gladioli. The air was sweet and wholesome, filled with winged flashes of color and the thrills of warbled song. As he meandered about the pleasant paths, he came upon a rushing fountain set in a marble basin. Its waters were thrown like sparkling jewels into the gentle air and were scattered into gems of iridescent vapor which fell into the basin. Here the clear water formed a shimmering pool dancing with goldfish and licked the soft pads of the lilies. When the wandering boy reached the brink of the fountain, he was overcome with a strong longing to remain where he was, and he sat down on the soft turf to enjoy the balmy air and the glory of the glittering spray.

As he sat there, a band of people came hurrying toward him, disrupting the calm peace of the park with loud cries and pitiful moans. They came staggering on until they reached the green grass on which the boy rested. Suddenly, they sank down on the earth as if in great weakness, and though they tried continually to reach the brink of the basin, they could get no nearer. The begging looks, the hollow eyes, the hanging tongues of the exhausted people moved the boy to help them. But when he tried to rise to give them a drink, he found himself rooted to the ground. He could not move to aid them.

For a long while he sat in anguish watching the suffering of the thirsty. Suddenly a great white bird swept down out of a tiny silver cloud, bearing a golden cup in its bill. It rested among the struggling sufferers, and Jacob saw the hands of two of them take the cup and lift it to their lips. Then there was a most startling transformation. Two of the party, those who had drunk of the golden cup, rose to their feet, seemingly restored to strength. But scarcely had they risen when a swirling whirlwind rushed upon them, swallowing up the entire group. When the roar of its passing had died away, Jacob saw that the two who had risen had been carried away by its irresistible power.

So terrified was Jacob by this supernatural occurrence that he cried out in great fear. His own cry awakened him, and he found himself on the floor of his father's cabin.

He immediately hurried to the side of the nearest patient, little Hendrik. Jacob bent over the dim form, felt his forehead and cheeks, and tried to give him water. At the first touch Jacob turned chill with fear. When last he had tended to the child, his forehead had been hot and dry, his cheeks had burned with fever. Then the little voice had whimpered for his mother, and his eager fingers had reached out for

Jacob's hand. But now his head was cold, his cheeks chill, his voice silent. No restless movement responded to the loving touch, not the faintest sound answered Jacob's anxious questions. The little heart lay still.

Jacob was panic-stricken. His brother Hendrik was dead. He had died while Jacob slept. In numbed weakness, he sat on the bed of moss and wept. How long he sat he did not know, but the flood of tears brought some relief. Fearful lest more dreadful things had happened, he turned to the remaining patients.

He was relieved to find his father sleeping, although feverishly, and his mother resting quite easy. Grietje, too, was still sleeping.

When he turned to the baby of the family, little Gerrit, he found the child open-eyed and lying very still. From his lips came a weak cry for mother. Jacob felt glad that there was evidence of life. He bathed his forehead with cooling water.

But when he lifted the tiny head and tried to pour the cool liquid into the small mouth, he was alarmed to note that the child's breath came in short gasps and that his body felt very limp and lifeless in his arms. He tried to restore the failing child, he cooled his face, he shook him gently, he called to him lovingly. But there was no use.

There had been no realization of death on the part of the child, simply a crying gasp, a little shudder, a closing of the eyes, and a falling asleep. A moment or two and little Gerrit was a child corpse beside his dead brother.

It was then that Jacob first saw death, stark, undisguised, naked. He had felt something of it before in the dying of others in the colony, but that had been different. It had seemed to be less fearful when an acquaintance had died, but now it appeared in his own family. His own brothers lay dead before him—Hendrik and little Gerrit—brothers whom he had loved and cared for, who now were gone away.

What made it worse was that he alone knew it, and there was no one else to support him in his grief or to share it with him. His father and mother lay helpless, incapable of knowing. If he could tell them and share his grief with them, he would feel better. If only he could lay the burden of his care upon his father's shoulders!

It was now early morning, and there would be other settlers about. Jacob was so stricken with grief that he never thought to call in any of his neighbors. He wanted only to tell his father and to be comforted by him. He wanted only to sit there by his dear family and weep until his eyes were dry and could weep no more.

After a time his loneliness and despair turned to desperation. He could endure it no longer. Flinging his hands into the air, screaming like a beast, choking in the outburst of his emotion, he ran from the room. The nearest neighbor was some hundred yards away, separated by a good stand of timber. Jacob did not go to him directly, as a sane person would, but he circled about, crying aloud and caring little whether he accomplished his purpose or not. It seemed as if his shouts and strange demonstrations gave him relief, for he found himself calmer in a few moments.

He looked toward the hut. He started and sickened with fear. There through the door, on the floor, he saw a leaping tongue of flame. The cabin was afire. The little light which he had lighted in the darkness of the dawn had fallen from the stand upon the floor and had ignited the dry material in his father's bed.

Jacob was taken with a paralyzing dismay. The troubles of the night had not been enough. Another peril must be added to it. Perhaps he must lose his father, or his mother, or little Grietje. The boy felt crushed, yet he knew the situation was desperate.

With a heart-rending screech, he rushed to the door of the cabin. On the floor, crawling about on his hands and knees, was Gerrit Kolf, dimly aware of the danger, yet too weak and too sick to do anything. Jacob was surprised to see how rapidly the greedy flames consumed the tinderlike bedding and reached with scorching tongues for the walls of the cabin.

His first thought was the safety of his mother. All thought of extinguishing the fire left him. He must bring his mother to safety. He hurried across the smoky cabin to the place where the sick woman lay. Struggling desperately, straining heavily with all his puny strength, Jacob half dragged, half lifted his mother from her burning bed.

He hardly noticed the strange figure that slipped by him in the murky dimness of the room. Yet when the figure passed him again, carrying his father, his heart leaped for joy. No sooner was Gerrit carried to safety, when the rescuer returned and gave Jacob a needed hand. Again he returned to carry out little Grietje, and finally the two tiny corpses.

When Jacob saw his relatives lying safely on the ground outside the burning cabin, he could do nothing but fall down beside them and give vent to his

91

feelings in uncontrolled tears. He gave no more thought to the burning cabin. But the unknown benefactor was more able to cope with the situation. He lost no time in re-entering the hut. Swinging a great cape of bearskin, he courageously beat out the licking flames until the last glowing spark was extinguished. He looked about him with satisfaction and saw that, except for the loss of bedding and a slight charring of the wall, no serious damage had been done.

His duty accomplished, the "Man in Bearskin" approached the huddled group of figures on the ground. A look of sorrow covered his face, and a hard swallow caught in his throat. What a spectacle! What a sad sight!

He bent over the sobbing boy and touched him gently. "Jacob," he said, "Jacob, be brave."

Jacob did not hear him until he had repeated his kind words. Then Jacob turned and looked up. A surprised expression, mingled with fear and delight, spread over his face as he saw his friend. "Sir!" he exclaimed, "Sir! Is it you?" And he clutched eagerly at his cape. "I thought—I didn't know—but I thought you were—well, I almost thought it was an angel."

The man could hardly find his voice to answer. "It was I, lad," he said, "and I came just in time." His words were thick with suppressed feeling. "Come, boy, we must get a new bed for the sick, and they must be put back into a sheltered place. It seems that you are in real need here."

Jacob remembered that his father had some material for bedding nearby, and he helped the man carry it into the cabin. The building was still livable. The smoke was cleared out as thoroughly as possible, and the patients brought back into the room from which they had been taken so hurriedly.

"This home has certainly seen more than its share of sorrow," said the "Man in Bearskin." "Tell me what has been happening here."

Jacob was not eager to discuss the train of misfortunes that had befallen his family, but his kindly friend encouraged him to relate them. In a voice unsteady with grief the boy recounted what had happened since last he had been at the enclosure in the forest.

The man listened with deep concern, watching with pity the signs of deep feeling as they played over the boy's features. When the tale had been told, the visitor arose and walked to where Gerrit Kolf was lying. He knelt on one knee and looked with intense sadness at the pale face and gaunt cheeks of the sick man. He lifted Gerrit's shrunken hand, stroked the back of it, then kissed it tenderly. His feelings began to overflow: his body shook, his head drooped upon his chest, and his great brown eyes were swimming with tears.

"It's bad, very bad," he said in a solemn voice, "and something must be done. Gerrit," he added, addressing the unconscious man, "Gerrit, you must not—no, you shall not die!"

Suddenly he stood up. "Jacob," he said, "why did you think that I was an angel?"

"Oh," answered Jacob, surprised by the sudden question, "I thought you were an answer to my prayer. I prayed that some helping angel might appear, and just then you rushed into the cabin, and carried my father out."

"Poor boy! I—an angel!" He lifted his voice to

express his utter disbelief. "No! No! Far from it! It was a happy coincidence that I happened along at just the right time."

"I don't think so. You didn't just happen to come. God brought you here because I needed you. It was an act of God. And I am glad. It shows me that He is still thinking of us and will bring us out of our trouble."

"No, boy. It's just this simple! I hadn't seen or heard of you for a long time and thought I would come to find out about you. I've been looking for that Indian rascal all this while."

"Did you find him?"

"No, I didn't. When I heard of the epidemic in Holland, I was anxious about you and your relatives, and came out early in the morning to see you. I was startled at your weird yelling and by your wild actions. When I saw the fire, I knew what was the matter and lost no time in getting here. That's all there is to it, boy—just a fortunate coincidence."

"I don't believe it," said Jacob.

"Well, never mind. We must get help for you, and medicine. I'll get some from Allegan and Wolf will bring it here."

"I'm afraid there is little help to be gotten in the village. Everyone is sick or has some relative to care for," suggested Jacob.

"I know it, boy, but I'll find someone." Without waiting to say more, the "Man in Bearskin" left Jacob and strode off in the direction of the settlement.

During the hour which followed before relief came, Jacob tried to arrange his scattered thoughts and to make clear the hazy impressions of what had taken place. As he sat in silence, not knowing what to

94

make of all that had occurred, Dominie Van Raalte entered.

Jacob was glad to see him. The fatherly man was surprised to hear the tale of misery and grief that poured from the lips of the lonesome boy. The minister examined the patients, gave them some simple medicine, prayed with Jacob for their recovery, and went away promising to send someone to help care for the sick.

A day later a genuine doctor and a woman nurse arrived. The doctor administered his remedies, the nurse gave the sick proper care, and in another day signs of recovery were evident in all three patients.

Each day the "Man in Bearskin" came within a short distance of the hut; from there he called Jacob to come and bring him news of the family. And when the boy was able to assure him that they would certainly recover, the man was clearly relieved and happy.

What need be said of the burial of the two children in the dark, moist ground? Their little bodies, wrapped in cloth, were laid away with a simple ceremony. The earth on which, for one short summer, they had run and played now received their small bodies to rest until some day a new life would call them from their sleep. A short, earnest prayer, a solemn psalm, a hushed reverence—that was all. The mourners were few—only Jacob, the Dominie, the nurse, and a neighbor family. But there was one mourner whom no one saw, standing aloof in the shadow of the forest, a tall strong man dressed in bearskin, viewing with sadness the simple proceedings before him, feeling in his heart a tenderness and a compassion that had not been there for many long years.

7

The bright days of the last of October had come as if to revive the deadened hopes of the Hollanders and as if to symbolize the cheerful future which would arise out of their days of trouble and sickness. It was on the last Sunday afternoon of the month that the "Man in Bearskin" sat on the knoll in the forest, resting in the full splendor of the fall day.

Although he had already lived in the woods for many months, no day had struck him with so much natural beauty. The air, still warm with the pleasant balm of summer, had in it the freshness of autumn. A mild breeze stirred the surrounding woodlands, the treetops dipped and swayed gently as if to pay their respectful homage to God who made them. Bright and clear, the blue sky seemed like a canvas stretched overhead, upon which was painted a scattering of silken clouds. The sun, golden giver of mellow warmth, shone with joyful cheerfulness. Its keen-edged rays darted in among the shades of the forest, danced fitfully on the crest of the oak trees, and chased the squirrel in his mad flights from the swinging maple.

The evergreen trees stood green and dull in contrast to the glowing leaves of the maple, gorgeously colored by the Divine Artist. The sweet scent of moist earth, the perfume of pine and cedar trees, lulled into dreaminess.

The whole world seemed to speak of peace and comfort. Yet for the "Man in Bearskin," who sat noting these things, there was no peace. Though his body reclined restfully on the green earth, his heart and his soul were tossed about by a great inward struggle.

He had not forgotten the dangers from which he had been delivered during the past summer. He had not forgotten his conversations with the young Jacob. He had not forgotten the terrible plight of the Kolf family and the almost miraculous way in which they had been saved. No, the events of the last few years were spun like a net which trapped his thoughts every waking hour and robbed him of sleep. The little funeral in the shadow, the simply burial of the two children had increased his anxiety. He could stand it no longer. His mind, his heart, his soul must be satisfied.

This afternoon he had resolved to settle the question. He would think about God; he would search his own heart and life; he would decide whether Gerrit and Jacob and Van Raalte were right when they talked about a God who was real and who was near.

It was odd that his thoughts should follow a different path from what he had intended. He had sat down on the ground with a spirit of growing despair. Then a mischievous little chipmunk, glistening in his coat of furry brown, strutting as if proud of his striped body, had popped out of a little hole from beneath the roots of a great tree and had sat, haughtily nibbling an acorn, before the man's out-stretched legs.

"You naughty little fellow!" he thought. "You seem to be quite satisfied with yourself and life in general. How unlike myself! All I know is bitterness and tears." Then the thought had come to him: "He is happy because he is doing what he was created to do; he isn't worried but is trusting, unknowingly, in his Maker."

The thought introduced a whole flood of memories. In his mind he was a boy again—a little Dutch boy, in dressed woolen pantaloons and jacket, shod in wooden shoes, whistling a funny little folksong, standing with hands in his pockets, gazing with wide interest into the little stream that ran through his father's village. He saw again the Dutch farmland, the little farm house, the rock pastures, the grey line of the distant dyke. He remembered his family gathered about the table, how his Christian father devoutly led in prayer, how, after the meal was finished, Father took down from the mantel the Holy Bible and read from it a whole chapter in a solemn yet pleasing voice, while the group of children sat around in respectful awe, hardly daring to move their heads lest they be scolded for not listening. He remembered the neat country church, built of wood, painted an immaculate white; how the country folk would gather there on Sunday mornings to hear the sermons of a dignified dominie who told them of their sins, of the shed blood of Christ and its power to save them, of the life that has no sorrow and no end for those who confess the resurrected Christ. He remembered Gerrit as a serious younger brother who was concerned about his older brother's evil ways, how he had hated Gerrit's warnings and correction, and how he had told him to mind his own business. Then he remembered a sad day when the body of his father was laid away among the dead in the churchyard, another day when the family wealth was divided and he received his share of gold coins done up in a little bag, and still another day when he closed his fingers on his brother Gerrit's share and like a sneaking, hunted thief made off in the night to a neighboring port to embark for America.

He shuddered to remember his base behavior, but he knew too that he was truly sorry for his dishonesty and that he had made every effort to make things right again.

He vividly remembered the whole series of dangerous events that had taken place since he began his life in the Michigan woods: how he had been trapped between the trees and was unexpectedly rescued, how the bear had treed him and nearly killed him, how he had narrowly escaped in other situations as he hunted or roamed the woods.

But the memories which caused him the deepest pain were those connected with the recent history of the Kolf family during the epidemic. The other things had concerned himself only; the sufferings and misfortunes of his brother and family were not so easily put aside. He felt a strong responsibility for the hardships Gerrit had endured, for the sorrow he had suffered in the loss of the little children. If he, the older brother, had not wronged Gerrit by taking his money, there would have been no need for such hardship and misery. Perhaps then there would have been no double grave under the moaning oaks.

If all this misery resulted from his crime of many years ago, why had he done it in the first place? He had to admit that he had taken the money, not because he was so greedy for gold, but because he disliked Gerrit who was always correcting him and pointing out his faults. Now, when he looked back, he had to question whether he was really justified in disliking Gerrit as he had.

Could it be, after all, that Gerrit had been right? Could it be that the God of the household Bible was really the Savior? How often his father had prayed that Christ would be his children's Savior too! Was Jacob right when he insisted that it was the watchful Father in heaven who had so often saved him from death?

Before, Dirk Kolf had felt only sorrow for his crime. He knew he had wronged his brother and that he must somehow repay him. But this Sunday afternoon he felt something new awakening within him. Sitting alone on the grass-covered hill, thinking about his life and its meaning, he came to see for the first time that he had sinned, not against his brother only, but against God. He had been wandering through life a sailor without a chart or a pilot without a compass. How was he ever going to make things right with God? He had lived as if there were no God. He had hated everything connected with religion; he had made fun of churches and sermons and prayers and the Bible. It was Christ, the Lamb of God, who took away sin. How many times he had heard those words! He wanted to pray to that Christ, but he had never really prayed before and he could not do it now. For a long time he sat staring into the aisles of the forest.

The sun of October had touched the western horizon. The dainty white clouds of the afternoon had thickened and were piling themselves about the golden ball as it dipped behind the fringe of trees. Now these great, fleecy arches, scalloped with delicate silver, took on the brilliant colors of the setting sun, crimson, pink, and gold. The forest was aglow in the dying sunlight. A hushed silence settled on the woodland. No trees stirred, no squirrel chattered; even the screaming jay lost its harsh voice. The "Man in Bearskin" drank deeply of the splendor around him. For the first time he saw that it spoke of the glory of God.

Faint, at first, from the distant village, came a swelling sound. The man became alert. What was it that he heard? Louder now and clearer, carried through the still air of the fresh afternoon, arose the solemn refrain of a Dutch psalm. It was the last psalm of the afternoon service in the log church of the colony. It was lifted from the throats of several hundred sturdy, devout Christians who had gone through a great crisis, and who now were worshiping their Everlasting God in thanksgiving for His care. The lone man in the forest recognized the song at once. His memory helped him hear the words as they floated across the open spaces.

Welzalig hij, wiens zonden zijn vergeven,
Die von de straf voor eeuwig is ontheven,
Wiens wanbedrijf, waardoor hij was bevlekt,
Voor 't heilig oog des Heeren is bedekt.
Welzalig is de mensch, wien 't mag gebeuren,
Dat God naar regt hem niet wil schuldig keuren,
En die; in 't vroom en ongeveinsd gemoed,
Geen snood bedrog, maar blank 'opregtheid voedt.*

*Psalm 32. The English version of this psalm is as follows:

How blest is he whose trespass
Has freely been forgiven,
Whose sin is wholly covered
Before the sight of heaven.
Blest he to whom Jehovah
Will not impute his sin,
Who has a guileless spirit,
Whose heart is true within.

While I kept guilty silence
My strength was spent with grief;
Thy hand was heavy on me,
My soul found no relief;
But when I owned my trespass,
My sin hid not from Thee,
When I confessed transgression,
Then Thou forgavest me.

So let the godly seek Thee
In times when Thou art near;
No whelming floods shall reach them,
Nor cause their hearts to fear.
In thee, O Lord, I hide me,
Thou savest me from ill,
And songs of Thy salvation
My heart with rapture thrill.

The man's straining ears caught the familiar sounds and took them in eagerly. When the last note had died away, and the impressive stillness of the woods only remained, he felt a great tumult in his soul. It was as if the stout limbs of the nearby oaks had bent down and lifted him up, holding him suspended in the airy spaces between the earth and the setting sun.

In his heart arose an uncontrollable emotion that choked him and brought tears to his eyes. They overflowed down his great rough face and into his thick, black beard. Now that his hard heart was broken, the flood of tears could not be checked. His whole body shook and rocked like a small boat on a open lake; his head drooped upon his chest as if it were too heavy for his sturdy neck. There was no help for him. Words spoken in the past, truths learned when he was a boy kept forcing their way into his mind and heart. They were too much for him.

When the last yellow ray had given up its gold to tinge the treetops of the horizon, and the grey softness of dusk had crept through the forest, the man had gone through a great change. It was not yet complete, but for the "Man in Bearskin" these first steps meant everything. From now on, his path was clearer before him, his step was surer, his course more certain. The heart that had been frigid and hard felt a new glow, a softness and tenderness it had never before known.

When night fell over the forest a new man arose and entered the hut.

8

The change which had taken place in the "Man in Bearskin" that Sunday afternoon was only a beginning. His mind had accepted God as real and the Bible as true. That should have made him see the whole world as God's world; it should have made a difference in the way he lived. But his life went on much as usual. There was little change in his behavior or his daily routine. It was clear that something more was needed.

He had prepared himself winter quarters by digging out a cave in the side of the hill and building in it a small, cozy dwelling of pine logs and hemlock boughs. To this new home he moved his meager household equipment and settled himself with Wolf for a long hibernation.

The weeks immediately following Gerrit Kolf's recovery brought with them a decided change for the better in the condition of the Dutch settlement. The medicine of the real doctors, the tireless work of Dominie Van Raalte and his corps of volunteer workers, and the continued fair fresh autumn weather all combined to bring about the stamping out of the plague and the return to life as it had been before the epidemic.

Gerrit Kolf, although deeply saddened by the loss of his two children, recovered quickly from the shock in the bustle and commotion of a busy life. He was a devout Christian, and he was satisfied to entrust his family's welfare to the Lord.

Jacob occasionally visited his friend in the forest. He could not understand why a man who was so wealthy would live such a simple, lonely life, but in all his conversation with the hunter, he was unable to discover the reason. Jacob noticed that the tribe of Indians had returned to the regions of Black Lake for a season at least, and he was quickly aware of the hunter's burning interest in the red men. Often when Jacob went to visit the dugout, he found the owner out on an exploration in the regions occupied by the tribe of Indians. Jacob gathered that the hunter had not yet given up his search for the beggar who had thrown from his pocket a soiled and crumpled piece of paper. The "Man in Bearskin" appeared to be unusually quiet and thoughtful these days. He acted kindly, but his mind seemed to be occupied with troublesome and disturbing thoughts.

In this way the long winter passed into spring. One day in early April the "Man in Bearskin" shouldered his rifle and strode off through the woods. Wolf, although openly eager to go along, was sternly ordered to remain at home.

"No, Wolf, let me go alone. I must be alone to think. If I could only find that money, I could be free to work out new plans, but until then—No! I must find it!"

The hunter tramped through the forest, deep in thought; suddenly he broke his chain of thought and looked about him. Try as he would he could not recall ever having been in the place before, although he had covered all the land within miles of his hut.

The trees, the earth, the sky, everything looked strange to him. He could see no way which would certainly bring him home. The way back was as unfamiliar as the surrounding forest. He knew that he was lost, but he felt no real alarm.

He decided to climb a tree in order to get a panoramic view of the country. Perhaps some familiar tree, some hillock, or known object, would give him a clue to his location. He chose as his post of observation a giant poplar whose tall, thin trunk lifted its head above the neighboring forest.

When he reached a vantage point in the treetop, he was amazed at the spectacle before him. A great field of green stretched off on all sides to meet on the south, the east, and the north the slightly hazy edges of the sky. On the west it was lost in the rolling sand dunes along the shores of the great lake. A vast sea of green, gently waving, moving on and on, being shaped by the slightest breeze—the endless stretch of woods filled the hunter with awe.

Having decided as well as he could the direction in which he should go, the "Man in Bearskin" descended and struck out through the forest. He had gone some hundred yards when, bursting through a thicket of young maples, he came upon two white wigwams. They were snugly set in the cool depth of the forest, away from the usual trails, in an out-of-the-way place.

His first impulse was to rush out and examine them more closely, but experience had taught him to be cautious, and he remained quietly where he was. As he watched with wide eyes and attentive ears, he hoped without knowing why, that this might be the home of the one he had been searching for so long—the Indian beggar who had dropped the crumpled paper. He knew enough about the habits of the Indians to know that these were the wigwams of a group of Indians who had broken off from the main tribe, possibly to carry on some independent, temporary work—perhaps to gather maple syrup, or to operate a trap line. Yet he knew that the Indians of this region were lazy and shiftless and that perhaps these wigwams stood there for no other reason than that their owners were too lazy to move them. The tribe was used to moving northward during the summer and spending their winter in the regions bordering Black Lake. A missionary, Reverend Smith, lived among them and had been successful in winning quite a number of converts. Most of the tribe had rejected the missionary's message and had clung to their gods, the Great Hare and the God of the Great Waters.

Because the wigwams stood among sugar maples, the "Man in Bearskin" decided that the occupants of the wigwams were probably sugar-gatherers. It was common for a small group of Indians to isolate themselves in a good stand of maples, there to drain the trees of their sweet liquid, collecting it in tin pails and boiling it in copper kettles. The brown-colored sugar was then put into baskets of birch bark where it was exchanged for clothing and food. To invade the territory worked by these sugar-gathering Indians was sometimes a dangerous step. They were suspicious of strangers and preferred to be left entirely alone. It was well known that one white man who had stopped at a sugar camp had never been heard of again.

The patient watcher was eager to get a closer look

at what lay before him, and in order to satisfy himself he moved forward cautiously. The change in his position allowed him to see a small fire behind one of the wigwams, and a copper kettle suspended over its blaze. A moment later he was happy to see a bronze-skinned man coming from the thicket on the opposite side of the little clearing, carrying a tin pail filled with sap. He approached the fire.

When the "Man in Bearskin" could see the Indian's features more clearly, he started violently. "The Beggar! That's who it is!" He was so shocked by the discovery that he remained powerless to act. He stood stock still in his tracks.

Suddenly he burst into action. He leaped from his hiding place and fairly flew at the now alarmed Indian. The Indian, stung by the fury of the oncoming man, dropped his bucket and awaited for the attack.

Without a word of warning the hunter sprang for the redskin. He closed his hands upon him in a powerful grip. "Beast," he cried. "Where did you get that piece of paper?" Then as if to present proof for his words, he released one hand and displayed a crumpled, dirty piece of paper.

"What do you mean?" stammered the Indian in very poor English.

"Mean! What do I mean! I'll teach you more plainly what I mean!" In the fury of his anger, he drew his fist and struck the red man a resounding blow in the face. "Perhaps that will jar your memory. I mean this paper—the paper you found wrapped around the bag of money you stole from me!"

The Indian was furious at the sudden attack. He

spoke not a word, but uttering a weird, unearthly scream, sprang for the hunter. Taken somewhat off his guard, the hunter was forcefully thrown to the ground. For a full moment the two rolled over the ground, locked in an iron embrace.

The call of the Indian had drawn from the woods four male companions who came running through the trees to the scene of the conflict. The hunter immediately saw his danger. His gun lay only a few feet from him on the ground. Putting forth an extreme effort, he broke the grip of the Indian, sprang from him, and grabbed the loaded weapon. Then he backed off a pace and faced the newcomers.

"Stay where you are, or I'll blow out your brains." The Indians, although they may not have understood his words, were certain of his meaning from his attitude. They were foiled by the white man's advantage over them and gathered together a few yards off to decide what to do next.

Unfortunately the hunter had not reckoned with his first enemy who, upon being released, had rolled rapidly to one side and had placed himself in a position somewhat to the rear of the white man. When he now saw the exact nature of the situation, he communicated a plan of offense with sly movements of his head and hands to the knot of companions some yards away.

Just as he was about to act, the white man noticed him and saw his own peril. He turned sharply, but the Indian had already dived for his legs. To train his gun on the diving Indian with any degree of accuracy was impossible. He aimed hurriedly; the shot rang out in the clearing; the rifle smoked harmlessly in his hand. At the same moment, the Indian's powerful body struck the legs of the white man and threw him off balance.

The fight that followed was desperate and terrible, but its outcome certain from the start. The four companions, taking instant advantage of the hunter's fall, rushed upon him. He was buried under a pile of fighting legs and arms. He struck, bit, gouged, and kicked, but the lean, sinewy fingers closed upon his throat; his strength ebbed and he was rendered powerless in the grip of many arms.

The commotion had attracted the attention of a squaw, who came out of one of the wigwams and drew near the group of struggling men. When the Indians had conquered their victim, they spoke to her in their own language, and in a moment, not too eagerly it seemed, she appeared with a coil of stout deer thongs. With these the Indians firmly bound the fallen hunter and left him tied on the ground while they gathered and talked in excited tones about various ways of killing the prisoner.

The hunter made sly efforts to free himself, but these only brought forth a stream of curses and gave rise to rough treatment at the hands of his captors. The question of what to do with him was soon answered. The party of red men finished their conference and once more gave their attention to the hunter. Picking him up bodily they carried him several hundred yards into the forest. Then, choosing a medium-sized maple, they bound him firmly, face outward, to the tree that was to be his prison.

The hunter was seized with the fear that they intended to dispose of him at once, violently. Therefore, when they abandoned him in the forest, taking leave of him with smirking grins and brutal looks, he felt that he was at least in no immediate danger.

Yet it took only a little while for him to realize that his situation was desperate. It was clear that the Indians planned to leave him to the slow gnawings of death by starvation, or as food for prowling beasts. His present position reminded him of his previous experience in the grip of the fallen trees and added to the terror which crept over him.

He began to feel the insane fear which had posessed him on the former occasion. His whole body shook with the chill of horror. The thought of night—dark, unbending night, of hunger with its unconquerable cravings, of thirst, the worst of all tortures possible to men, with its swollen tongue, its cracked throat, its burning eyes that will not close—all these thoughts sapped his courage and made him weak and overcome with dread.

The night would be cold, for it was early spring. The creatures of the forest would be abroad to terrorize him. His bound muscles would become cramped and aching. The thongs of deerskin—how they would cut! And the chafed wrists—how they would burn!

When the first hour or two of captivity had passed, his mind turned to different thoughts. After all, the suffering would be short, and misery, if it is short, can be endured. But after the suffering—what then? Death, from which there was no escape! Death!

Yet when he came to think about death, he was not so terrified after all. He experienced a greater calm than he had ever felt before when his life had been in danger. Somehow he felt he deserved the punishment he was receiving, that it was a fitting end for the life he had led. He had lived carelessly, godlessly, selfishly. He had invited trouble; now it was here. Let him drink to the bitter dregs the cup he had poured for himself. He was satisfied that he was getting what he deserved.

But that was not enough. Even if it was just that he die in this way, what then? He was content to die if death was what he deserved, but what would death bring with it? He tried to think it out.

His Christian training had taught him that faith in God and sorrow for sin would bring him everlasting happiness. But he had ignored God; his life had been evil, and he had never asked for forgiveness. How would he escape the horrors of hell?

In his extreme distress he prayed as he had never prayed before. His prayer was simple, but it was enough: "O God! My Holy God! Show me what I must do! The way ahead of me is black and I can't see! Send me a ray of light!"

It was remarkable that he did not pray to be set free from the thongs that bound him to the tree. They were forgotten because greater cords bound his soul—the stronger bonds of sin.

After that first agonizing burst of prayer, the man felt great relief. Now he poured out his troubles like a swelling stream, and a burden was lifted from his soul.

It was almost dark before he again began to think about his peril and the possibilities of escape. The rapidly gathering dusk, the growing cold brought back something of the earlier fears and terrors. He studied the way in which he had been fastened, hoping to devise a way to free himself. He examined the cords to see if he might cut them somehow. He tried to reach them with his teeth, but he could not. His struggles failed to break them, his efforts were absolutely unsuccessful in loosening the least bit the sinews that held him fast. He dared not call lest he attract some wild beast to the place where he was tied. He knew well enough that there was no hope that anyone would hear his call if he did raise his voice. He could only wait and hope for what seemed impossible.

Long after dark he heard a strange sound—the moving of a large body through the forest nearby. His fears multiplied instantly. There was no doubt of it. Something was moving there. There was the sound of a soft footfall. What could it be?

Perhaps his captors were returning to enjoy the anguish of their victim. Perhaps they had come to do what they had not dared to do in daylight—to murder him brutally and to gloat over his bleeding body. Whatever the thing might be it was extremely cautious in its approach. It seemed hesitant and wary. After each footstep there was a long pause. Perhaps he was only imagining the sounds! Or the visitor may have gone away altogether!

The man was so filled with suspense at this uncertainty that his lips moved in a whispered prayer. "O God!" he sighed, "O God! Help me!" His body quivered with the earnestness of his appeal.

"I come!"

What was that? A human voice, speaking English? "I come!" The unexpectedness of the reply took the breath from his body. Who came? Why did it come? His eyes strained eagerly to pierce the surrounding night. But he could see nothing; no form separated itself from the shapeless black of the forest.

"Who comes?" he shouted in impatient anxiety.

"Are you afraid, white man?" was the answer. In a moment the hunter could see that the voice belonged to an Indian woman.

"Who are you?" he asked.

"Let not the white man be afraid." responded the woman in a kindly voice, speaking English.

"Are you one of the Indians?" asked the captive, by the tone of his voice that he meant those who had captured him.

"It is so," she responded. "It was Mastaki who found the thongs of the deer that her husband might bind the paleface."

"What is it you want?" asked the hunter, expecting nothing good of her.

"Mastaki has come to cut the sinews!"

The full import of these words were lost on the man. "Who told you to?" he asked. "Why do you release me?"

"No one has told Mastaki, but she feels the suffering of the paleface and has pity."

Still suspicious of the true intentions of the woman, the hunter continued. "What do you expect to do with me? Aren't you satisfied to leave me to die? Are you alone?"

"The heart of Mastaki is true and deceives no one. She has come to free the white man and she has come alone. The knife is in her hand. She will cut the strong cords. She will save the brother of Christ." The simplicity and sincerity with which the squaw spoke impressed the hunter and filled him with hope.

To his intense joy she came to him and without a sound severed the thongs of deer hide that bound him. His limbs fell free. His position had been so

114

cramped that he could not now support himself, and he fell in a sudden heap to the ground. He was so dazed by the unlooked-for change in his fortune that he didn't know whether to shout or weep.

"You are free," said the woman, "but neither the birds, nor the trees, nor the tongue of the paleface must whisper the name of Mastaki."

His gratitude toward the woman knew no bounds. He could not understand why she should have been so kind to him, and he could only look upon her action as an answer to his prayer for freedom. The man was deeply moved by his deliverance. Outwardly he appeared to be calm, but inwardly he breathed a fervent prayer of thanksgiving.

"Why was the paleface so filled with fear while Mastaki crept through the forest?" asked the woman simply.

"Woman, I saw death—certain death—before me and who would not be afraid? But tell me now, why did you care to free me? I have done you no favor."

"But, white man, did not the Jesus tell Mastaki to love her brothers and sisters, and to help them?" The squaw seemed puzzled that the hunter did not understand.

At the name of Jesus, the "Man in Bearskin" started. Jesus! He had seldom heard that name used by anyone except other Hollanders. How strange it sounded coming from an Indian squaw! He had not thought that Jesus could mean anything to an Indian, or that the power of Jesus' gospel could affect the conduct of a squaw.

"So you are a Christian?" he asked in surprise.

"It is so, paleface! Once I bowed down to the gods of my fathers, but a white man came among us. He

115

told me that the waters were not gods, that the Great Hare and the sun were made by a greater God. He said that the Great Father sent out His Son, not to fight on the warpath, or to slay the buck and the wildcat, but to be a shepherd to feed the sheep. He said we were the sheep and that the Shepherd feeds us. When we love the Shepherd, then we will be loved by Him. He said that we should love also the other sheep, and that all Christians are sheep. Why then should not Mastaki love the white man, since he is a Christian? Why should not Mastaki steal away from the wigwam of Oshtobi, who is a wolf, to cut the bonds of the captive? Does not Mastaki do only what the Great Father has told her to do?"

The man was struck dumb by the woman's words. To think that a squalid, wild squaw should have been so greatly influenced by the teachings of Christ that she should feel kindly toward all Christians, that she should have endangered her life to do him an act of kindness. The flush of deep shame spread over his face, and the man hung his head.

"The white man must have been greatly wronged," continued the woman. "Did Oshtobi steal his children, or did he shame his wife? What has Oshtobi done that the white man should try to kill him?"

Without answering her question the man asked one himself. "Is Oshtobi your husband?"

"No. Oshtobi is my husband's brother."

"And is he also a Christian?"

"The water has been sprinkled on his forehead, and he has said, 'I believe in Jesus,' but in his heart he loves not the Savior. Oshtobi is a wolf. What did he do that you are angry with him?"

"I do not know whether Oshtobi has done me hurt or not, but I believe he has."

"It is strange that the Christian white man should try to harm him who has done him no ill."

"I am not certain, woman, whether I should tell you what the trouble is." He hesitated to tell his secret to a strange squaw, yet he felt that he could trust her, and perhaps she might help him in some way.

"Do you know," he asked, "whether Oshtobi has much money?"

"Oshtobi and the dog depend upon others for food and shelter. He had some shining gold pieces, but they are gone."

"Where did he get them?"

"He said the heart of a white man was softened when Oshtobi saved his life."

"What did he do with the money?" asked the hunter, feeling that he had a clue.

"He went to the white trader and drank firewater. His legs were trembling like the stricken deer, and he talked strangely like the screaming loon."

"How long ago did this all happen?"

"It was in the time of the blossoming maple, in the spring of last year. Oshtobi left us when the North called. We thought the long sleep had overtaken him, for we saw nothing of him for many moons. But he finally came back."

"How did he carry the money?"

"A little bag wrapped in paper was his purse."

"A bag! In paper! Are you sure? A little bag in paper! It sounds only too true. Oshtobi did not get the money from the white man. He stole it from me."

"But where did he steal it? Where does the pale-face live?"

In a few words the hunter explained the whole matter—how he had buried a sack of money to keep it safely, how it had disappeared from the spot in which he thought it had been placed, how he had searched about hoping to come upon it, how the beggar had accidently dropped the telltale piece of paper, how he had chased and tracked the Indian for many miles and many days without finding him, how finally he had hit upon the sugar camp and recognized the beggar and how in the fight that had followed he had become a prisoner.

"But," interrupted the woman, "Oshtobi did not have many gold pieces."

"No, most of the money was in bank notes. They were wrapped in skin. Perhaps he did not recognize them as being valuable and threw them away. If he did, I am lost, for I'll never be able to recover and restore the money."

"But why does the paleface weep for the loss of his money? Does he make it his god? Mastaki has no money. She has only the flesh of the deer and the fur of the mink and the fox. But she is happy, for she has Jesus for a God. Does the paleface need more than Mastaki?"

The man was too ashamed to answer. Yet he felt the need to unburden his heart.

"Woman, you seem to believe that I am a good Christian. Your faith is so pure and simple that you expect me to be Christlike just because I am white like your missionary. You must know that I was a wolf like Oshtobi, a thief and a robber."

The squaw was surprised by the confession of the

118

white man. "Does the white man not know that Jesus has died for the thief and the robber? Does he not know that the Christ will forgive the wicked man? Why does not the white man pray? Then he will be happy. Then he will find his money. Then he will forget his grief."

"Daughter of the missionary, you are right. I know it deep down in my heart, but I can't seem to accept it and live it. My faith is so weak."

Then the squaw did the unexpected. "I will pray for you." She dropped on her knees and simply said, "O Jesus, lover of the sinner, of the white man and the red man, hear the prayer of Mastaki, the sorrowing one, of Mastaki who loves Thee and believes in Thee. Help the paleface, Jesus, to love Thee. Help him to live like Thee. Help him to find his money. Let him see that the words of Mastaki are Thy words; that Thou art good like the warming sun and the falling rain. Jesus, touch the heart of the paleface and let in the colors of the rainbow."

She spoke as a child to a father. Her words were deeply sincere, and pleasant voice was made beautiful by the earnestness of her plea. When her prayer had been said, she stood up and would have spoken to the man. But he was himself on his knees and he was praying. The example of the Indian woman had been too much for him. Her tender faith, her unshaken trust had put him to shame and had made him more aware of his own need.

His prayer was warm and came from his heart. "Jesus, my God, my Savior! O God, take my sinful heart and make it clean through the blood of Thy Son. Help me to serve Thee! I am sorry for my theft and I will repay the debt. I will follow after Thee!"

The squaw looked with pleased expression at the kneeling man. When he arose, she spoke to him. "It is good that the white man has found Jesus."

It was almost morning, and the squaw said she must leave. She had been thoughtful enough to bring with her a portion of Indian cornbread and a piece of smoked venison. These she gave to the man, with kindly words for his welfare.

It was useless for the man to express his gratitude. "It was for Jesus' sake" was all she said in answer to him as she slipped back into the night.

9

It was Sunday morning in the little Dutch settlement. A bright, peaceful calm lay over the colony as if to symbolize the peace of God which comes to those who worship Him. The work of the week, the plowing, the woodcutting, the home-building had been laid aside completely. There was a hush over the land—a hush as if to reverence the presence of God.

It was the day of rest and worship for the Hollanders, and all the inhabitants were preparing to attend the services in the little church in the cedar swamp. No one stayed home except those who were very ill. It was the day on which the children's hands and faces received an extra scrubbing, their clothes a careful brushing, their shoes a special polishing. It was the day on which the good Dominie Van Raalte spoke to his people, urging them to live a pure, simple, honest Christian life.

In the home of Gerrit Kolf the Sabbath preparations were in full swing. Little Grietje was busy helping her mother clear away the remains of breakfast; Gerrit sat on a crude seat reading the Bible.

"Father," said Jacob, "I wonder what ails the 'Man in Bearskin.' I have gone there twice to visit him, and neither time was he at home. His dog seemed hungry and I fed him, but it seemed as if the man

121

had not been home for a long time. He's acting very strange these days, and I'm almost becoming afraid of him."

"He is a strange man," answered Gerrit, looking up from the Bible. "I often think of him and the favors he's done for us. It's sad that he should spend his life in such a lonely, useless way. Maybe something in his past is troubling him, and he doesn't have the courage to face it and straighten things out. If we only knew what it is, we might be able to help him. Has he ever said anything that might give you a clue?"

"No, Father, but I believe you are right."

The conversation turned to the affairs of the household while the family finished its preparations for church. Promptly at the usual time the little group, Bibles in hand, started out for the log building where the Word was preached.

But the Kolf family was to miss services for the first time since the frightful epidemic. Gerrit was about to open the door when someone knocked. Before the opened door stood the "Man in Bearskin."

"I must come in," he said.

The family re-established themselves about the room, looking with curious eyes at the stranger of whom they had so recently spoken. Everyone seemed embarrassed and uneasy. No one said anything. Gerrit stared intently at the guest's partially hidden face. There was something vaguely familiar about it. If the man would only throw off that robe, perhaps Gerrit might recognize him.

To Jacob, who knew the visitor better than the others, the "Man in Bearskin" seemed greatly disturbed. There was a wild, eager look in his eyes, a nervous twitch to his jaw. His face was flushed and seemed thinner than usual. He gave the impression of being keyed up to a high pitch of nervousness as if in preparation for a trying ordeal.

Jacob first found his tongue, "Sir," he said, "are you ill?"

"Not ill, Jacob, but miserable," came the answer. Something in the voice startled Gerrit. What was that familiar accent? "It is the curse of God that has pursued me, and now I have come to satisfy it. Gerrit Kolf, do you know me?"

The bearskin robe fell from his head and shoulders. Gerrit turned ashen pale, his eyes bulged in their sockets, he caught his breath. He arose from his place and almost staggered to the man of mystery. "It is so," he cried. "It is Dirk! My brother!"

The scene which followed was touching. Two strong men, who usually did not show their feelings, gripped each other's brawny hand, embraced each other warmly, and wept. They were tears of joy, of sorrow, of forgiveness. The heart of the thief was melted by the warm, pardoning embrace of the brother he had wronged. Neither spoke. There was no need for words. The hunter's tremendous relief and Gerrit's warm-hearted welcome were feelings too big to be expressed.

It was some time before the two reconciled brothers could recover sufficiently to take their seats. The rest of the family, expecially Jacob, looked on, marveling at what they saw, hardly able to grasp the meaning of it, gazing with a kind of blank awe at the remarkable scene.

Jacob was dazed by the revelation of the fact that the mysterious stranger with whom he had been so friendly was none other than his own uncle. He could not contain himself in his excitement, and fairly pounced upon the now smiling hunter.

At last the family calmed down a bit, and they settled themselves to talk about what had happened and to get used to their newly established relationship.

"It was the curse of God," the hunter repeated, "that followed me from the shores of the Netherlands across the wide ocean to these wild regions. I thought I could be happy with the money, I thought I could quiet the voice of conscience, but each passing day saw me more miserable. I tried to overcome my growing unhappiness by living a wild, self-centered life. I spent my fortune on luxuries to forget what could not be forgotten. It was all useless. I became convinced that I could not be happy until I restored the money to you. But when I made such a resolution, I found it hard to carry out. I set to work to regain the amount I had taken from you, and I was able to do that. When at last I had accumulated the ten thousand gulden, I learned that you had sailed to America. It was some time before I was sure of your coming to Michigan, and as soon as I was certain, I decided to find you and give back the money.

"Unfortunately I had become afraid of losing the regained money, and very foolishly buried it to keep it safe. When you arrived, I tried to express my good will to you secretly, fully intending to reveal my identity in a few days. But my plans went awry. When I went to dig up the buried money, I found that someone had been there before me, and the money was gone. I couldn't find it, although I scoured the neighborhood forest and dug up the earth under every tree in the vicinity of the one where I thought I had hidden the money. My failure to recover the money made me bitter toward everyone and everything. I felt that until I could ʼestore the money I could not face you and expect forgiveness.

"The months passed without my getting one bit nearer the discovery of the money. I ran into dangers and escaped from them. I kept track of your activities and became acquainted with Jacob. The secrecy in which I had to live angered me. Everyone looked at me as a stranger and an enemy. I felt that I was doing all I could to restore the money I had stolen and that this was very noble of me. The fact that I was prevented from carrying out my plans set me against God; I thought it was His fault. I never had been religious and never had much use for Christ, but when I lost the money, I hated God and cursed His name.

"Then I learned of the beggar and the slip of soiled paper. Perhaps Jacob has told you about it. I was determined to find him. It became a passion with me. I dreamed about the Indian wretch and the crumpled paper night and day. I followed the slightest scent. I ran down every clue, but the sly fox escaped me, and I became more desperate, more embittered with each failure.

"It was in this crisis that God brought about a change in me. I began to think about my guilt, my efforts to repay my debt, and the many ways in which my plans to do so had failed. I remembered the old home, the old church, the old Bible. And when I heard the strains of Psalm thirty-two sung from the church here in the colony, I underwent a change.

"It dawned on me that I did not have to deal with you first of all, but with God. And how was I to repay God? When I became aware of my sin against God, then I also remembered Christ's message of forgiveness. I turned to Him, and He gave me peace and salvation."

The man paused for a moment to recover his self-control. His words were clear, but his voice had became almost a whisper. Then he continued by recounting his capture by the Indians, his trying experiences in the forest bound to a tree, the kind act of the Indian squaw and her fine Christian conduct.

"It was too much for me," he said. "I felt that I must forget myself and the money, reveal my identity, and endure the consequences. I have no payment to offer you, only a heart filled with sorrow and remorse. If you can forgive, I will work to repay. I will find money somewhere, and you will not suffer for having lost what I have taken from you."

"Dirk," Gerrit said softly, "I have nothing in my heart for you but kind thoughts and forgiveness. I am doubly happy that my money has helped you find a richer treasure. Surely my ten thousand gulden were a cheap price for the soul of a brother."

The morning passed quickly; the brothers shared memories, Dirk became acquainted with Gerrit's wife and the children, and the two men talked about the colony and their plans for the future. At noon they gathered about a table set with coarse but wholesome food, and their hearty appetites showed

126

that the two men were completely at peace with each other.

In the afternoon, Dirk Kolf, the "Man in Bearskin," attended church for the first time in many years. It is said that sounds of surprise could be heard all through the congregation, but Dirk's humble, worshipful behavior made it clear to everyone that he had a perfect right to share in the simple worship of the God whom he now claimed as his own.

10

Dirk Kolf came to live with his brother, and Wolf, who had been forgotten for a time in the excitement, was brought to live with his master in Gerrit's home.

The now happy hunter felt that the only way in which he could repay his brother for keeping him in his household was to furnish the table with meat. It became his custom during the few hours in which he did not work about the village to take his dog, and, in company with Jacob, track down the wary deer and the fleet rabbit.

On one such occasion the little party came upon a flock of wild doves flying swiftly overhead. Jacob had recently acquired a new shotgun and asked his uncle if he might try it on the doves. In an instant he had aimed the gun and discharged the shower of leaden pellets into the group of flying birds.

A dozen birds fluttered hesitantly and fell to the ground. Jacob, elated at his success, quickly began to gather up the game. He discovered that one of the birds had fallen into an old, snarled oak and had been caught in its branches. One bird in twelve seemed only a small loss, yet the boy wanted them all. He began to climb the tree.

He was surprised to notice a peculiar hole in the

side of the trunk, which formed a perfectly hidden pocket in the tree. His curiosity was further aroused by a furry object which seemed to have been pushed inside the hole. Cautiously Jacob reached in and drew out an odd-looking bundle wrapped in the fur of a small animal.

"Uncle Dirk!" he shouted. "Uncle Dirk! Look what I've found," and he threw the bundle at the feet of the man on the ground.

His uncle's cry was so shrill that Jacob released his hold and fell to the ground.

"The money! The money! Thank God! I've found it!" The man seized the parcel eagerly and opened it. Inside was a neat bundle of bank notes kept from harm by the protection of the skin.

The joy of the hunters was unbounded. They danced and jumped and pounded each other almost into tears. The dove in the tree was forgotten, and when Jacob arrived at home he found that he had lost several more on the way.

The recovery of the money was a great help to the struggling family of settlers. They were able to buy for themselves a fine tract of good farmland, to build themselves a larger home, and to hire the necessary men for farm labor. Dirk remained with the family and hired himself out to his brother.

The hardships which had made Vrouw Kolf eager to return to the Netherlands were now past, and she was happy to remain in the colony. The advantages of living in the new country seemed clear; the family knew now that their dreams would come true.

The Kolfs and their neighbors had shown their

courage and their trust in God; He blessed them, and their colony became the thriving city of Holland, a growing settlement in the Black Lake region of Michigan.